RUMAYSA

A FAIRYTALE

RADIYA HAFIZA

ILLUSTRATED BY RHAIDA EL TOUNY

MACMILLAN CHILDREN'S BOOKS

Published 2021 by Macmillan Children's Books
an imprint of Pan Macmillan
The Smithson, 6 Briset Street, London EC1M 5NR
EU representative: Macmillan Publishers Ireland Ltd, 1st Floor,
The Liffey Trust Centre, 117-126 Sheriff Street Upper,
Dublin 1, DO1 YC43
Associated companies throughout the world
www.panmacmillan.com

ISBN 978-1-5290-3830-9

Text copyright © Radiya Hafiza 2021
Illustrations copyright © Rhaida El Touny 2021

5 7 9 8 6 4

A CIP catalogue record for this book is available from the British Library.

Printed and bound by CPI Group (UK) Ltd, Croydon CR0 4YY

For the lights in my life, my nieces and nephew

A, H & L

CONTENTS

Rumaysa

I

Once upon a time, in a land quite far away, snow was falling heavily from the dark sky, blanketing the land of Splinterfell in white. It was a night full of promise to some, for the first day of snowfall marked the beginning of winter and the coming of festivities and joy. It was time to shut up windows, spend time with loved ones and retreat from the outside world.

Not everybody could take part in such joy, though. There were some families who had less than others, and the fall of snow meant a definite end to the hopes of crops and work.

There was one family who were particularly less fortunate than others. Naina lived in a little hut on the outskirts of the village and spent her days sewing clothes for wealthier ladies.

Her husband, Samar, was usually gone for most of the day, trying to find work, but he never had any luck. Some said his bloodline was cursed to poverty. Others cruelly and unfairly whispered that he was a bad worker, so nobody would hire him.

When Samar returned home one night after another long, hard day of searching for work, his hands were once again empty. Naina began to weep, tired from her day of stitching, with nothing to eat since morning. She feared for her unborn child; there were only two more moons to go until the baby came. Unable to bear seeing his wife so upset, Samar went back outside in search of food.

Over the hill, right by the edge of the woods, there was one house to which nobody ventured too close. The dark wooden building was surrounded by different crops and berries in the garden. It was said the Witch of Splinterfell lived there – though nobody had ever seen her – and that anyone who stole from her bounteous garden would have to pay a price. What that price was, no one could be sure, but few were willing to take the risk to find out. Samar, however, was desperate. He snuck his way over to the house and slipped in through the large gates that encircled it.

Samar felt as though he had stepped into a dream. There were all kinds of fruits and vegetables growing in the Witch's garden. He stood in uncertainty for a moment, and then began to take as much of the food as he could carry. He ran back to his house, looking over his shoulder all the while. He spotted no sign of the Witch nor anybody else.

Naina was overjoyed when Samar came home with the food. She turned the vegetables into a stew and they ate merrily, with the fruits for dessert.

The next evening, Samar returned home again having had no luck in finding work. He hesitated before entering his house. Through the window he could see his wife lying in bed, cradling her large stomach. He gazed at her for a moment, making his decision.

Samar snuck back into the Witch's garden and took all he could carry again.

The Witch didn't seem to exist. So Samar returned again and again over the next two months, taking whatever food he could find. Naina began to glow with health and, soon enough, the time came for their child to arrive.

The birth of Naina and Samar's baby carried on through

the night and day. Finally, the baby came screaming into the world. Naina and Samar were weeping and laughing from exhaustion. It was a girl. They called her Rumaysa.

Just as Naina was holding her daughter for the first time, joyfully cradling her and stroking her cheek, a knock sounded on their wooden door.

'Who is it?' Samar called.

'It is I,' came a low voice. 'The one from whom you have been stealing.'

Samar froze. The hairs on his body stood up.

'Who is that?' Naina asked, clinging her baby tighter to her chest.

'I don't know what you are talking about!' Samar cried, frantically searching for some sort of weapon – but their small house was bare.

The door swung open with a loud *smack* to reveal a figure cloaked in black. All they could see of her pale face was dark red lips and a pointy chin.

Samar's eyes widened in horror. It was the Witch.

'For two moons you have stolen from my garden,' the Witch said. 'Now I have come to take what is mine.' She lifted a skeletal finger and pointed at the baby.

'No, you can't,' Samar said, paling with fear. 'That's our baby!'

'You should not have stolen from me. You know how the old song goes, don't you, Samar?'

Samar was terrified. How did she know his name?

He knew the song – everyone in the village did. But he thought it had just been another children's rhyme.

The Witch began to sing, cackling:

> *Under the dark moon, the Witch's garden blooms.*
> *Take what you will from the trees or the ground*
> *But she will take your first seed to sprout.*

It was a terrible song, not catchy at all, but Cordelia (for this was the Witch's name) seemed to think it was inspired.

'No, please—' Samar begged, but the Witch silenced him with a snap of her fingers. She strode over to Naina and snatched the child from her hands.

'No – my baby!' Naina cried out. 'Please! You can't take her!' She struggled to get up. 'Please!'

'Too bad, dear,' the Witch hissed. 'She is mine now.'

'No – *Rumaysa*!' Naina fell out of her bed, struggling towards the Witch. Cordelia cackled and slammed the door on her way out, disappearing with the child into the night.

'No!' Samar roared, his voice suddenly returning.

'Samar, we have to do something!' Naina screamed.

Samar could barely think. He desperately ran outside, trying to see which way Cordelia had gone. Up above, he saw what looked like a bat in the night, flying away towards the moon. He blinked and the silhouette was gone.

Panic coursed through him. 'No! No! *No!*' he screamed, clutching his hair. Samar ran towards the Witch's house, through the brambles and boughs that led to the edge of the forest. But when he reached the house he'd so often visited, it was gone.

He stared around in shock. The land on which the Witch's house used to sit was now just a charred patch of ground. There was nothing but burnt grass and ashes. Samar's knees went weak and he fell to the ground in despair.

In the distance, a cackle echoed in the air.

II

One dark and dreary night many years later, a young girl named Rumaysa was sitting in a small tower room lit by candlelight, working with straw and a spindle. The young girl sang a particular song as she hunched over the wheel, the long hours of the night filled with her soft melody. It was a curious thing, spinning straw, but something odd happened while Rumaysa worked. With each moment of her song, the straw she spun turned into gold.

The gold shimmered with the flickering light, but the room was still rather miserable to look at. The large spindle took up most of the space in the centre of the creaky oak floor, framed by a wooden bed and a cracked stove and sink. A small toilet at the back of the room had been curtained off with an old blanket. The only thing that was remotely nice were the piles of books stacked up against the cobblestone walls. The Witch who held Rumaysa captive had given them to her from a young age – it saved her having to speak to the girl too much.

Rumaysa stopped singing as the edge of her frayed sleeve caught on her dark wooden spindle. She frustratedly pulled it off the spinning wheel, but it still created a new tear in her greyed and well-worn dress. She sighed in annoyance and continued working.

She was a scrawny girl whose golden skin had a deathly pallor to it – probably because she'd been trapped in a tower her whole life. Her sharp face could probably cut something if you asked her nicely, and she wore a simple grey hijab on her head. Her eyes were big and honey-brown, sparkling with a fierce energy as she concentrated.

There was a rustling at the small window where the wisps of moonlight streamed into the tower through the thick trees outside. Rumaysa jumped, nearly dropping the straw in her hands, worried that the noise announced the arrival of the Witch.

But it was a beautiful owl that swooped into the bleak room. Her feathers were ruby red and glistened as though they were on fire.

'Rumaysa!' the owl hooted in greeting.

Rumaysa breathed a sigh of relief. She put down the straw and stretched her aching fingers. 'Hi, Zabina. Was the coast clear?'

'Not a witch in sight,' replied Zabina. She glided over to drop some berries in the girl's lap.

'Thanks!' Rumaysa exclaimed. 'Where did you get them from?' Her stomach gave a loud grumble as though asking the same question.

Zabina settled herself on the edge of Rumaysa's bed. 'From the bushes by the river. I was going to get some nuts from the *other* side of the river, but the wind was a bit fierce today.'

'You're the best,' Rumaysa said gratefully, throwing a handful of the fruit into her mouth.

'I know,' Zabina replied, bowing with her wings spread out.

Rumaysa's tower was surrounded by thick, ugly trees with branches that were spiked with sharp red thorns. No creature that lived outside these cursed woods dared to enter for fear of the Witch. The exception was Zabina, who was nosy enough to pry in the first place and small enough to fly around without being seen.

'So, what's the news from the outside world?' Rumaysa asked through another mouthful of berries.

'*Well*, it appears that the foxes have been stealing food from the wolves, and then Faruk the jaguar found out his sister is

12

going to elope with a tiger, so there's a lot going on in the big cats' quarter . . .'

Rumaysa listened intently to Zabina's monologue on the forest gossip. The owl lived in a much less frightening jungle in Whistlecrook, where plenty of creatures roamed, mostly peacefully. Apart from her books, Zabina's speeches were Rumaysa's only real glimpse of life outside the tower. She soaked up every word, imagining the colours of the different creatures, how the rubble of the earth felt under their paws, the wind in their fur – the freedom.

As Zabina continued talking, Rumaysa got up from her seat to sweep the floor. She gathered the mess from around her spindle and threw it outside her window. The trees that surrounded her tower seemed to bristle slightly as the straw cascaded around them.

Turning back from the window with a shiver, Rumaysa asked, 'What else have you been up to today?' to distract herself.

Zabina looked at her pink talons. 'Well, it just so happened that I saw Dana as I was getting the berries.'

'Oh, so that's why you went to the riverbank,' Rumaysa said knowingly, raising an eyebrow. Zabina was currently nursing a very serious crush on a raven in the woods. She began gushing while Rumaysa laughed and sat back down at her spindle.

Now, you might be wondering what on earth a girl was doing speaking to an owl, and really there is no other explanation besides magic. Many years ago, an entire forest had suddenly sprung up in the middle of nowhere, encircled by a thick, bubbling river laced with poison. What used to be a swathe of fields along the western plains of Whistlecrook was now full of thorny sky-high trees. Grey clouds hung permanently over the woods, and the townspeople whispered that the forest was full of evil.

The King of Whistlecrook had tried to get the forest torn down, but no boat could make it through the cursed waters. Many workers had found misfortune in its dark depths. Eventually, the King had given up. As no trouble came from the new woods, it was left alone, and the townspeople kept away.

Nobody knew that in the very centre of this cursed forest was Rumaysa's tower, where she had lived all these lonely years.

For the fruits that had grown in the Witch's gardens were laced with strange magical properties. As Naina had consumed them while with child, Cordelia knew that Rumaysa would carry magical powers, and so she kept the girl in a tower, forced to spin gold, day after day.

After all these years, Rumaysa still wasn't certain what the Witch did with the gold. Zabina thought that Cordelia consumed the gold to stay immortal. Rumaysa supposed she used it to live a wealthy life.

Magic is a strange thing. And Cordelia knew how to work it to her benefit.

III

The next morning, Rumaysa did her prayers and sat down to mix the rest of Zabina's berries with her usual breakfast: oats. Every month, Cordelia left Rumaysa with a large sack of oats, and, unsurprisingly, Rumaysa was sick of them. She was practically drooling at the purple colours in her otherwise beige bowl.

She propped a book open as she ate – *The Conference of the Birds*, in case you were wondering – and, once she'd finished eating, she settled herself at the spindle. Rumaysa siphoned off the straw with her putty knife and turned it into soft hairs to weave through the needle on her spindle. As she began to sing, she felt the light hairs turn into heavy threads of gold. She spun and she spun, her fingers moving quickly and precisely. She worked all day, her back becoming stiff from her wooden chair.

As the sun began to set, Rumaysa suddenly noticed that she could see her breath coming out before her. The air had turned icy. The hairs on the back of her neck stood up.

'Romsara!' A high-pitched cackle followed the intentional mispronunciation of her name. Rumaysa looked up in dread as the Witch appeared by her window. She flew in through the opening, landing silently on the floor with her black boots. Her face was hidden by a hood, just as the rest of her figure was cloaked in dark fabric. Tall and willowy, she loomed over Rumaysa as if she were one of the trees in her woods.

'Hurry up! I haven't got all day,' she snapped.

'Yes, Cordelia,' Rumaysa said, shivering. She hated the extra chill that Cordelia brought to the air. She quickly grabbed the bag of gold by her spindle and hauled it over to the Witch, hoping that she would leave quickly.

Cordelia looked around the small tower room distastefully. 'Why don't you ever clean up in here? This place smells like a stable.'

Rumaysa looked around. Her room, as always, was spotless. 'I will,' she said through gritted teeth.

17

'Good. If you need some rags and soap for cleaning, you only have to ask, you know. Honestly, child, you might clean yourself up a bit too. All that dirt on your face.'

Cordelia reached out a pale hand and Rumaysa flinched as the cold fingers wiped a smudge away on her face.

When the Witch next spoke, her voice was softer. 'There, much better.' She suddenly smiled at Rumaysa, showing her sharp teeth. 'I got you a present.' She drew a book from inside her cloak and handed it to Rumaysa. It was called *100 Recipes for Oats*.

Rumaysa forced herself to smile. She took it, murmuring, 'Thank you, Cordelia,' as she did.

'I'll bring you some things for cleaning tomorrow.' Cordelia clicked her fingers and the sack on the end of her broom came floating towards them, landing at Rumaysa's feet with a quiet thump. 'Here's more straw for you to spin. Have it ready by tomorrow evening.'

Rumaysa stared at the bag – it looked like there was almost double the usual amount of straw. 'Cordelia . . .' She steeled herself. 'I-I'm not sure I can finish all that by—'

Cordelia narrowed her yellow eyes and snapped her fingers, silencing Rumaysa. The girl moved her lips, eyes wide with panic, but no sound came out. Her voice was gone!

'You will have this straw turned into gold by tomorrow evening,' Cordelia said in a dangerous voice.

The Witch snapped her fingers again and Rumaysa gasped, clutching her throat, as she was released from the spell.

'Yes, Cordelia,' Rumaysa whispered in a hoarse voice.

The Witch smiled again, her sharp teeth gleaming once more in the candlelight. She picked up the bag of gold and mounted her broomstick. 'I'll be back tomorrow, Rumseera,' she sneered over her shoulder.

Rumaysa sighed with relief as the air returned to its normal temperature. She sat on the edge of her bed, staring miserably at the large sack of straw. She had half a mind to chuck it out of the window. Straw, straw and more straw! Her tower may as well be a stable.

Rumaysa grumbled to herself and set to work at the spindle once more. 'Is she building a fortress with all this gold?' she muttered to herself. 'Why on earth does she need *so* much?'

When she had worked through a quarter of the bag, Rumaysa was exhausted. She did her night prayers and got ready for bed, putting on her sleeping gown and weaving her long, dark hair into a plait.

Rumaysa refused to let sleep take her drooping eyes just yet. She opened up her favourite book, *One Thousand and One Nights*. It had beautiful drawings of palaces and animals, women in hijabs and men in magnificent robes. It was a relief to step into someone else's life and escape her tower room, if even just for a moment.

It was the only book Rumaysa owned where the characters had similar names to her and shared her skin colour. All her other books had names like Cordelia's. The pages of her copy were well worn; it was her most treasured possession.

She had also found a small book inside it with instructions on how to pray five times a day. Rumaysa liked how the prayers broke up her day, giving her something to do in between spinning straw. She didn't think Cordelia had meant to give it to her, but she was glad for it.

Rumaysa wondered what other books were out there in the world. If she ever got out of the tower, maybe she could have her own library. She smiled at the thought, imagining walls lined with books. But then her face fell.

When will *I get out of here*, she wondered for the millionth time. Rumaysa sighed and got off her bed. She traipsed over to the window and looked outside at the forest.

Rumaysa had, of course, been trying over the years to escape the tower. She knew that hers was not a normal life. Zabina had tried carrying her out – which had quickly failed – she'd tried screaming for help for hours until she'd lost her voice. She'd tried pretending to be ill so she could go and see a healer, but Cordelia had just told her to stop complaining.

Zabina had flown far and wide, for days on end, to try and find help. But, of course, any time she came across a human all they could hear was Zabina hooting – Rumaysa was the only one who could understand her.

The trees before her tower bristled, as if sensing her thoughts. Their dark trunks and thorny branches seemed to huff and puff in the wind, almost as if they were drawing themselves to their full height. An eerie whistle sounded in the air as the wind blew through the leaves.

A branch snapped.

Rumaysa jerked her head up and saw it falling from a tree. Out of nowhere, another branch whipped out and grabbed it, pulling it silkily back into the thick of the forest.

Spooked, Rumaysa stepped back and closed her window shutters once more.

Rumaysa liked to daydream – or nightdream, you might call it at this hour – and imagine a world beyond the forest, beyond these four walls. She was a princess fighting battles out in the fields, saving her people from destruction. Or she was a baker in a cosy shop, in a village where everybody knew everyone's business. An ocean explorer with a glittering magical fin for legs. The dreams went on and on.

But at the end of all of them, Rumaysa would return home to her parents. She dreamed of food on the table, maybe bread and hot soup (definitely no oats), and she would spend dinner telling them all about her day. And then, as the night wound down, her parents would tell her endless stories to send her off to sleep.

But they were only dreams.

IV

Before the sun had even risen the next morning, Rumaysa was already up. She needed to finish the bag before Cordelia arrived. Sunrise came and went, the high noon faded into the setting sun, and her back and arms ached desperately for relief.

Rumaysa pushed on, trying to get as much gold spun as possible before nightfall.

As the sky bled out into purple and blue, Rumaysa's eyes drooped. She stifled a great yawn, leaning back against her chair in exhaustion. She just needed a moment to close her eyes . . .

'Romsara!'

Rumaysa jolted awake. She let out a small involuntary

shriek at the sight of Cordelia looming over her, red lips pulled back in a snarl. The Witch's eyes narrowed as she took in the spinning wheel between them, half strung with straw and gold. 'Why isn't my gold ready?' she asked in a low voice.

Rumaysa's stomach fell as she looked outside the window. The sky was pitch black.

'I'm sorry – I fell asleep – I was tired,' Rumaysa said, her words tumbling over one another. Panic was shooting through her.

'Asleep,' Cordelia repeated. 'The whole day?' Her voice was rising. 'For what? Why could you possibly be so tired? Lazy child!'

Rumaysa didn't reply; her hands were trembling as she tried and failed to wrap the straw through the spindle.

Cordelia looked around the room, her eyes zeroing in on the books by the bed. 'Up reading late, were you?' she sneered. 'I don't mind you having some fun, Rumaysa, but not when it interferes with my work! I clothe you and feed you and keep you safe, and all I ask in return is you make my gold on time!'

Rumaysa didn't dare speak. Her stomach twisted with nerves and anger.

'But no – apparently I'm asking for too much!' Cordelia spat.

'I'm sorry, Cordelia!' Rumaysa said, trying to keep her tone even.

'Sorry is not good enough,' Cordelia snapped. She clicked her fingers and immediately all Rumaysa's books rose slowly up off the floor. They hovered eerily in the air, turning on their spines.

'No, wait!' Rumaysa gasped, dropping the straw and lurching out of her chair. 'I can finish the gold; I just need a bit more time!'

'Tough,' Cordelia snarled.

'Cordelia, please!' Rumaysa begged, looking desperately at her floating books. 'I'm sorry! I promise I won't let it happen again!'

Cordelia looked at Rumaysa with great contempt before snapping her fingers once more. The books exploded into a flurry of torn pages, coating the tower room in fragments of parchment and leather.

'No!' Rumaysa cried. She dropped

to the floor and desperately grabbed some of the torn paper in her hands. They broke away into dust.

'This is what happens when you disobey me,' Cordelia said in a steely voice.

'But I didn't disobey you!' Rumaysa said frantically. 'I just — I just fell asleep! Please, please put them back together! I promise I won't do it again!'

Cordelia glowered at her. 'I will not reward your incompetence!'

Rumaysa couldn't bear to look at Cordelia. Angry tears welled in her eyes as she took in the fragments of paper covering the greyed wooden floor.

'I'll be back tomorrow night. Have my gold finished!' Cordelia hissed, turning on her heel.

Rumaysa keeled over and bit into her knee, refusing to cry,

but a terrible
sob broke
through. The reality of her unjust life
was far too great to bear. What had she done
to deserve this?

Apart from Zabina, her books had been her only
company in this miserable tower.

And now they were all gone.

As Rumaysa stared around,
the tears started to stream down
her face, and a glint of purple caught her eye. She
grabbed the piece of paper. It was from her favourite
story in *One Thousand and One Nights*: the story of
Shahrazad. The piece Rumaysa held in her hand showed a
part of Shahrazad's face, wrapped in a purple hijab. An angry
scream ripped out of Rumaysa's throat
at the sight of the broken queen.

She wanted to break her
spindle, tear it apart piece by
piece, and throw it outside to
the cursed woods. She wanted to
tear apart the straw and burn the

gold into nothing. But she was helpless.

After what felt like hours, Rumaysa dragged herself back to her spindle. Tears fell silently down her cheeks as she worked, dropping on to the straw as she ran it through the spindle and sang her song. The straw glowed as it morphed into pure gold, gleaming in the candlelight.

Dawn eventually broke, filling the tower with soft purple-and-pink light. Rumaysa heard a flapping near the window.

'I've got pears!' Zabina sang. 'I had to fight a beaver for them, but –' She stopped short at the sight of Rumaysa's room. The fruit fell from her talons, thudding on to the wooden floor.

She gasped. 'What happened?'

Rumaysa wiped her face hastily. Her eyes felt raw from weeping. 'I fell asleep yesterday and didn't get all the straw finished,' she croaked. 'Cordelia destroyed all my books.'

'Why, that evil witch!' Zabina said angrily, flying over to Rumaysa. She landed softly on her lap and patted her comfortingly with both her wings. Rumaysa felt as if she were in a feathery hug.

'I wish I could get you out of here,' Zabina said sadly.

'You and me both,' Rumaysa mumbled.

Zabina looked at Rumaysa. 'Are you OK?'

'I'm fine,' Rumaysa said curtly.

'Rumaysa?' Zabina prompted.

Rumaysa seemed to deflate, her shoulders sagging as she sighed. 'I'm stuck here forever, Zabina. There's no point pretending I'll ever escape.'

Zabina hooted unhappily and flew up, hovering in front of Rumaysa at eye level. 'That is not the Rumaysa I know. You *will* get out of here one day!'

Rumaysa ignored her, got up from her chair and traipsed over to the window.

Zabina continued, 'We just need to come up with a plan. There must be *something* we can do . . .'

Rumaysa leaned her head against the cold wall, closing her eyes. Quietly, without even realizing what she was doing, she started humming to herself. A sad tune that told of lost moments and love. She wondered again about her parents and what kind of life she might have had with them. Were they still out there? She longed for them with all her heart.

When she opened her eyes again, she realized her song had brought a trail of fireflies up to her tower. They hovered before gently floating in, twinkling like golden lights in her gloomy room.

She reached out and cupped a few of them in her hands. The tiny flutter of their wings felt ticklish in her palms. Rumaysa carried on humming as she sat back down at the spindle, her once-dull room now lit up with a ceiling full of glittering stars.

V

The next day, Zabina was determined to cheer up Rumaysa. 'I have something for you!' the owl announced as she perched on the window ledge.

Rumaysa looked up, her face void of interest. 'What is it?' She tried to smile. Her mouth sort of twitched.

'It's a scarf!' Zabina said proudly, pulling a piece of gold fabric from behind her back with her talons. 'Thought you might like a new hijab.'

Rumaysa's brown eyes widened in surprise. She got up to go and get a closer look. 'Wow, it's lovely,' she said, feeling slightly cheered. She reached for the scarf, curious to see what it felt like. It looked so silky and soft.

As Zabina passed it over, a gust of wind caught the fabric

and it slipped from Rumaysa's fingers out of the window.

'Oops,' said Zabina.

Rumaysa had to lunge, grabbing the end of it before it fell away. Half hanging out of the window, she looked down, momentarily mesmerized by the gold fabric spilling down the tower wall.

She gazed at the hijab for a few moments, and then dazedly drew herself back inside, clutching the scarf to her chest. Her heart began to pound, faster and faster.

'I have an idea,' she said slowly.

'What? What is it?' Zabina asked.

'I'm going to escape,' she breathed. '*I'm going to escape!* Zabina, you're a genius!'

'I'm confused, is what I am,' Zabina hooted.

'I'm going to make a hijab!' Rumaysa declared.

'Well, no, dear – see, I already got you one,' Zabina said slowly, gesturing at the scarf in Rumaysa's hand.

'No, not like this!' Rumaysa burst out. 'I can make a different hijab! More like a rope!'

Zabina looked on in surprise as Rumaysa walked towards the large bag of straw by her spindle. She could do more than turn straw into gold. Or less.

Rumaysa needed to be smart. She could take a small amount of straw every night, just enough so that Cordelia wouldn't notice, and she could use it to make a new hijab. A very long hijab that would reach from her tower window to the forest floor.

Zabina was watching her curiously with her wide blue eyes.

'It might take a while, maybe a whole month. The tower is ridiculously high . . . But if I can spin some gold threads into the hijab, it will be strong enough to hold my weight as I climb down the tower! Maybe I can finally escape this prison and go and find my parents!' Rumaysa said excitedly. 'I need to figure out how long the hijab has to be, though. Do you think you could check?'

'On it!' Zabina squawked, swooping gracefully out of the window. Rumaysa watched as the owl disappeared downward.

'Are you at the bottom yet?' she shouted down after a few moments.

33

'Nope!' Zabina called back.

Rumaysa waited another minute. 'How about now?'

'Nope!'

'Really?' Rumaysa grimaced as she looked at the sack of straw. This was going to take a long, long time.

But, even with that grim thought, Rumaysa had never been so excited to spin straw. She practically leaped across the floor to her spindle, exhilaration coursing through her as she began to work. She sang as she spun the long, golden threads, and then worked in silence as she spun the rest into normal yarn. Rumaysa then twined the plain and gold strings together, knitting them so they began to form a thick, strong scarf.

When she had used as much as she dared, she hid the beginnings of her hijab under her pillow and began her work for Cordelia, thinking all the while. It took all of her will not to take more straw from the bag that first night, but she couldn't risk the Witch noticing.

When Cordelia returned the next night, Rumaysa waited

with bated breath as the Witch took the sack of gold. Her heart pounded in her ears as Cordelia seemed to consider the bag for a moment. But she left without a word.

Rumaysa sighed with relief as the cold left the tower along with the Witch. She ran to her pillow and looked at her scarf. It was about the length of her torso, a delicate blend of white and shimmering gold.

As she stared at it, she couldn't help wondering whether her plan would actually work. And, even if she could escape, getting out of the tower wouldn't be her only problem . . .

When Zabina came back the next day, Rumaysa didn't even say hello. 'Zabina, how big is the forest?' she asked instantly.

The owl glided from the window ledge to the bed. 'Very big. I've been thinking, if you can't fly over it, you'll have to go through it, and then there's the river . . .'

Rumaysa felt a knot of fear tighten in her stomach as she went to the window. The sun was setting, but even on the horizon nothing but the dark treetops were visible. When it was really quiet, sometimes she could hear the faint gushing of the venomous river that snaked around the bewitched woods.

'The trees are her spies,' Rumaysa said in a quieter voice,

almost afraid they could hear her. 'Do you think I can make it past without waking them up?'

'Don't suppose you could make yourself some wings instead?' Zabina suggested.

Rumaysa looked back at her with a grimace.

VI

Days and days passed, and Rumaysa felt that her scarf
would never be long enough. It was tiring spinning
gold during the day and trying to make her escape scarf at
night. Though she supposed she didn't have much else to
do, now that all her books were destroyed, and Cordelia
continued to seem none the wiser about the missing
gold.

Every night Rumaysa measured the scarf with Zabina, who
would take off from the window ledge and shout, 'Rumaysa,
Rumaysa, let down your hijab!' chuckling to herself as she did.
Rumaysa had read a similar line once in a book, and Zabina
could not stop laughing about it.

Every night she prayed that the scarf would reach the

ground, but Zabina would always return to say that it wasn't long enough.

About a month after she had started to make her scarf, Rumaysa was unceremoniously awoken by Cordelia looming over her. She held back a scream. 'Cordelia, what are you doing here?' It was early in the morning, way too early for the Witch to be here.

'I brought you breakfast, Rosmadara,' she said, brandishing a blueberry muffin.

'Er, thank you,' Rumaysa said confusedly. She held back a flinch as her fingers made contact with the Witch's icy cold skin.

She could see the Witch watching her expectantly, so she hesitantly took a bite of the muffin. It didn't taste completely awful.

'I have to go away on some business, so I will not see you for a few days.'

Rumaysa looked up in surprise. 'Where are you going?'

Cordelia narrowed her eyes distrustfully before answering. 'Very soon, we will be living in a new home. Together.'

Rumaysa blinked a few times. 'What?'

The Witch smiled wolfishly. 'All this gold you have been making over the years, I have been moulding it into many

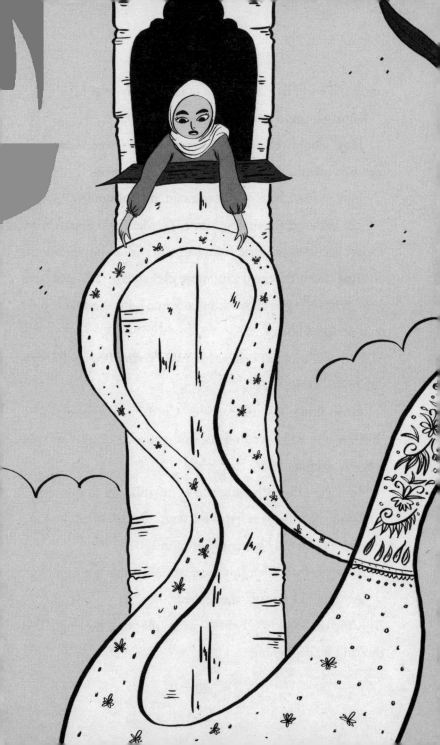

things. We will live in a palace made entirely of gold.'

Rumaysa could only stare at her in shock.

'How would you feel about leaving this tower, Rumaysa?' Cordelia asked silkily, her yellow eyes lighting up.

'I get to leave here?' Rumaysa said, dumbfounded.

'*Yes*, with me, to our new home,' Cordelia said impatiently, apparently annoyed that Rumaysa was still asking questions. She had clearly expected a bit more excitement. 'You will have a room fit for a princess, with many fine possessions and your own personal library.'

Rumaysa couldn't believe her ears. 'You've been building a palace this entire time?'

'Great things take time, child,' Cordelia said importantly. 'But no one will ever find us, and you will be able to spin straw in a much finer setting.'

Rumaysa's stomach sank. She would still have to spin straw?

'Won't that be wonderful for you?' Cordelia said, looking around distastefully at her tower room.

Rumaysa forced her lips to move. 'When do we leave?'

'As soon as I return,' she replied.

Rumaysa couldn't believe what she was hearing. This couldn't be happening.

'I've brought three extra sacks of straw. Do one a day, and I'll be back on the fourth night to collect them – *and you!*' She laughed, seemingly inspired by her own humour.

The knot in Rumaysa's stomach tightened. 'Yes, Cordelia,' she said quietly.

Rumaysa watched the Witch leave, but even after the cold had dispersed she sat transfixed on her bed. Cordelia was going to take her to a new prison. One Rumaysa had helped make.

Rumaysa couldn't go. She wouldn't! She had to leave.

She had four days before Cordelia would return, and a whole load of extra straw. She had everything she needed to complete the scarf.

When Zabina arrived that afternoon, Rumaysa was covered in straw and felt a little worse for wear, but her eyes were wide with feverish excitement.

'What's going on?' Zabina asked.

Rumaysa filled her in on Cordelia's news.

'A palace?' Zabina hooted in dismay. 'We need to get you out of here!'

'I'm leaving,' Rumaysa said. 'I've got four days to finish this scarf. And I *will* be done by then.'

VII

Three long nights passed as Rumaysa wove her magic scarf together. She had barely slept, and she was sure her aching hands were about to fall off. But at last the scarf was ready.

'Psst,' Rumaysa hissed out of the window. '*Psst!*'

For a moment, the darkening sky was silent. Then there came a rustling in the trees.

'Oh, it's just freezing tonight,' Zabina's squeaky voice called.

Rumaysa stood back as the owl flew in through the window. 'Now is not the time to be worrying about the weather!'

Zabina twisted her head from side to side disapprovingly. 'It's a good thing you're leaving – I don't know how you'd survive another winter in this awful place!'

Rumaysa hoped she wouldn't have to either. She was practically bursting with excitement and fear. 'Are you sure the coast is clear?'

'Yes, yes, I checked the edge of the forest, and then I checked *over* the forest, then I watched *past* the hill – she's definitely gone.'

'Great. Great. That's good. This is good.' Rumaysa was bouncing with nerves. She hurried to her bed and pulled out the long golden scarf. After tying one end securely to her bedframe, she started to lug the rest of it over to her window.

'That is the world's finest hijab,' Zabina said proudly.

'If anyone ever needs a million-foot-long hijab made, send them my way,' Rumaysa replied breathlessly.

She heaved the last of the hijab out of the window. As she watched it fall, its golden threads shimmering in the moonlight, she held back a terrified gulp. It was so dark down below; it was impossible to see where the scarf finished. She really hoped the bedframe would hold her weight.

'Don't worry – I reckon you'll only break a few bones,' Zabina said comfortingly.

'Thanks,' Rumaysa said. She looked back at her room one last time. It was now or never.

Rumaysa lifted herself up on to the ledge and swung her legs over, holding tight on to the scarf. Zabina flew past her head and hovered outside.

'OK, here goes,' Rumaysa said, gently lowering herself over the other side. She felt a chill go up her back as the cold night air welcomed her to the outside world.

'How far down is it, Zabina?' Rumaysa gulped.

'Um, you haven't even moved,' Zabina replied.

Rumaysa didn't dare look down. 'Right. Moving. OK. Move.' She breathed. 'I can do this.'

Her flimsy grey shoes slipped a few times as she tried to get a footing on the tower wall, but after a few moments she began her descent. Immediately, she heard the bed loudly scraping across the floor towards the wall, and for one scary moment, Rumaysa thought it was all over. But the bed steadied and her scarf stayed firm. It felt sturdy enough for now. She continued to climb down.

'I can't believe we're doing this!' Rumaysa shrieked in a whisper after a few moments.

'Come on, hurry!' Zabina fretted, looking all around them.

'I'm trying to!' Rumaysa snapped back. 'Why don't you climb down a gigantic tower and see how fast you go!'

Zabina was quiet for a moment. 'Come on, you can do it!' she began cheering instead.

When it felt like she had been climbing for hours, Rumaysa sneaked a glance downward. She wished she hadn't – all she could see was an unending ocean of black and the tall, thorny trees around her, drooped in their slumber. She forced herself to look back at the tower wall and took several deep breaths. Her arms felt like they were on fire.

'Hello?'

Rumaysa froze. Zabina's head darted all the way round in terror.

'Hello? Is anyone in this tower?'

'Who is that?' Zabina hissed worriedly, taking flight towards the trees to look.

It was a boy's voice calling.

Rumaysa looked down, her heart pounding in her chest. She couldn't see anything distinguishable. 'Hello?' she called back nervously. *Who was that?*

'Hello!' the voice replied, sounding relieved.

'Who are you?' Rumaysa asked, worried that it was a trick from Cordelia.

'I'm Suleiman, from the land of Farisia!' called the voice.

Rumaysa had never heard of it. Though she hadn't heard of many other places, to be fair; she didn't really get out much.

'Tell him to be quiet – he might wake up the forest!' Zabina said.

'Please be quiet!' Rumaysa called in a low voice.

'Sorry!' the voice called back in hushed tones.

'Why are you here?' Rumaysa demanded, struggling to keep her grip. Her arms shook with the weight of holding on to the rope, the burning ache in her muscles intensifying.

'I'm looking for someone – a princess. Have you seen her?'

'No, I'm the only one here,' Rumaysa replied tersely.

It was quiet for a moment. 'Right, OK. Guess I'll go, then.' Rumaysa heard an odd whoosh in the air and then silence. She let out a breath of relief – the boy must have gone.

As she restarted her climb, she muttered, 'When I need someone to break me out, no one shows for years and years. But the night I'm hanging from a sky-high tower, *then* some boy wants to show up.'

Zabina hooted in shared contempt. 'Come on, Rumaysa!

You need to hurry!' she said in a whisper.

Rumaysa nodded and moved quickly downwards. In her haste, she was half climbing, half slipping, causing her body to scrape against the grey stones. She was sure her hands would fall off from the burning pain searing through them.

As she clambered further down into their eerie shadow, she felt the trees start to rustle, as though they were yawning . . . or waking up. The air shifted suddenly, turning even colder. Panic shot through Rumaysa again, making goosebumps erupt all along her arms. She had to hurry.

'Almost there!' Zabina whispered eagerly.

Rumaysa started to feel a sense of relief and she risked another look down. She could actually make out the ground beneath her!

She eagerly hurried down, but in her rush her hands missed a beat and she lost her grip on the scarf. She yelped as she scrabbled to grab it, slipping a few feet. Rumaysa managed to grip the scarf again,

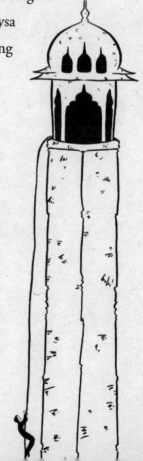

her heart pounding in her ears as she held on tight with relief.

But as the scarf pulled taut, an ominous crash sounded from above. Rumaysa felt the fabric slip again as her bed frame came flying out of nowhere, and she went plummeting down into the dark, screaming as she fell.

VIII

*C*rash!

Rumaysa landed with a hard thud on the soggy grass.

'Ow,' she moaned.

'Rumaysa! Rumaysa, are you OK?' Zabina swooped down after her.

'I think I'm broken,' Rumaysa said feebly as her entire body throbbed with pain. Her head spun as she struggled to see through the stars in her eyes.

'Can you get up?'

'I think I'll just lie here,' Rumaysa croaked, trying to find all her limbs.

'I don't think you can,' Zabina said anxiously. 'Come on – we need to go!'

Rumaysa sat up groggily. The world was still spinning, but at least it seemed like it was slowing down. She was starting to become aware of how cold she was.

She stumbled to her feet, leaning on the tower wall for support as her vision steadied. She looked around, suddenly realizing what she had achieved. *She was outside!*

Excitement coursed through Rumaysa as she took in her surroundings. On the ground, the trees looked even taller than they had from her tower. Some barks were thin and spiky, others were bulky with knots on the trunks, but they were all coated with the dangerous red spikes, so like the Witch's red lips.

She shivered in the cold night air, pulling part of her hijab down from her shoulders to wrap around herself like a blanket.

After taking a deep breath, she said, 'Let's go.'

She headed towards the trees, still marvelling at the dark forest. The leaves fanned out above her head, allowing only slivers of moonlight to come in. All kinds of ferns covered the bottom of the tree trunks, laced in and around the thorns. She was taken aback by the sheer vastness of it all.

There was a thin layer of snow on the ground, and Rumaysa's shoes were getting soaked through. Every step she took crunched, but thankfully the trees stayed asleep.

Rumaysa had been walking for several minutes when she heard an odd whooshing noise again – it was coming from behind her. She turned round and almost screamed, clamping her hands over her mouth in fright.

'Sorry, me again.'

There, right in front of her, was a boy on a floating red rug. Rumaysa gasped, blinking a few times. This outside world was very strange indeed.

'What does he want?' Zabina whispered from beside her.

The boy looked uncertainly at Zabina, and Rumaysa realized that all he would hear was a low hooting noise.

'What do you want?' Rumaysa asked in a quiet voice.

'Sorry, I'm just lost—' the boy began loudly, but Rumaysa cut him off.

'You need to be quiet!' she hissed. 'These trees might wake up. And make sure you don't touch them.' She was not going to let this boy ruin her plan, after weeks of spinning her escape.

He looked around them uncertainly. 'Um, are the trees alive?' he asked in a hushed voice.

'They're enchanted by a witch,' said Rumaysa tersely.

'Wow,' Suleiman looked shocked. 'Um . . . I don't know where I am – I really am quite lost. Do you know anything about a stolen princess?'

'Rumaysa . . .' Zabina said warningly, ushering the girl with her wings.

'I don't,' Rumaysa said, turning her back on him. She really didn't have time for this. The Witch could come at any second.

Rumaysa started walking again, quicker than before, but the boy trailed behind her on his carpet. 'Wait!' he called quietly after her. 'Maybe I can help you. Where do you need to go?'

'I need to get out of this forest – and so do you.'

'Well, can I give you a lift?'

Rumaysa stopped between two dark trees with thick trunks and turned back towards him. He was gangly with brown skin and had dark hair that flopped wildly around his round face.

'We can fly on my carpet over the forest. Surely that's got to be quicker than you walking through it?' he said earnestly.

She had to admit it did sound more tempting. Rumaysa narrowed her eyes at him, considering whether he was really trustworthy, and it crossed her mind for a moment that he could even be the Witch in disguise. She reasoned that Cordelia didn't have the patience to play these sorts of games with her – and, anyway, it wasn't as cold as it normally got when she was around.

Rumaysa walked towards the boy, scrambling up on to the piece of floating material.

'Be careful,' warned Zabina, her eyes narrowed suspiciously.

'It's OK, Zabina,' Rumaysa murmured to her.

'Tell him to get above the trees and head north,' Zabina said.

Rumaysa relayed this information back to the boy.

'Right.' He nodded, still looking confusedly between her and the owl. The rug seemed to respond of its own accord and began to lift them upwards. Rumaysa held on, awed by how carpet slipped through the branches, towards the night sky, expertly dodging the dangerously sharp thorns.

'I'm Suleiman, by the way,' the boy said again.

She focused back on the boy. 'I'm Rumaysa, and this is Zabina,' she replied.

''Where did he get that carpet from?' Zabina asked suspiciously.

Rumaysa quietly asked Suleiman the question. Her stomach gave a flip as she spoke – she suddenly realized that she was talking to another human being!

'I made it,' Suleiman replied, sounding very proud. 'Well, sort of. I repaired it. I found this old rug in our attic and patched it up, and – well, it turned out it was a magic carpet!'

Rumaysa was impressed. A magic carpet sounded like something from one of her books. Although she reasoned that perhaps she shouldn't be so surprised; she could turn straw into gold, after all.

'What are you doing in these woods?' Suleiman asked Rumaysa, as the carpet manoeuvred around a particularly large branch.

'I'm escaping an evil witch,' she whispered. 'She stole me from my parents when I was a baby. She wanted me for my magic.'

54

Suleiman looked frightened, but Rumaysa's thoughts had turned back to Cordelia. 'Do you think she knows we've gone?' she asked Zabina.

'Not yet, but she will,' Zabina said, flapping worriedly as the carpet continued to navigate its way through the spiky trees.

'I've never actually met someone magical before,' Suleiman said excitedly, forgetting to whisper.

'Shush!' Zabina snapped.

Suleiman looked at the hooting owl.

'She said to be quieter,' Rumaysa said.

'I don't know what he's doing here in the first place,' Zabina grumbled.

'What did she say now?' Suleiman asked in a hushed voice, his eyes wide with wonder.

Rumaysa hesitated. 'Er, she asked who you're looking for.'

Zabina gave Rumaysa an affronted look.

Suleiman's face fell. 'A princess. I've never actually met her. She was taken by a dragon months ago, and no one has seen her since.' Suleiman did not sound particularly grieved.

'Don't you want to find the Princess?' Rumaysa asked curiously.

Suleiman looked alarmed. 'Of course – it's just . . . I like fixing things. I like being in my den. Being outside and exploring all these strange places is a bit scary, if I'm honest, but my parents think this is what noble boys should do . . .'

'He's just trying to make you feel sorry for him,' Zabina said petulantly. 'He's probably taking us to this dragon!' She hopped threateningly towards Suleiman as the carpet continued its ascent, her blue eyes narrowed angrily.

'Is she OK?' Suleiman asked, leaning away from the menacing owl.

'She just wants to get out of here,' Rumaysa said sheepishly, pulling Zabina back.

Zabina glowered at her, puffing out her feathery chest.

'So, what brought *you* to these woods?' Rumaysa asked, trying to change the subject. They lurched as the carpet leaned right, narrowly avoiding a twisted branch.

'A different type of magic, I guess,' Suleiman said, taking a necklace out from inside his cloak. A small oval stone hung in the centre, glowing purple in the dark. 'This is meant to take me to the Princess, the one most in need, but I keep ending up in different places with no sign of her.'

Rumaysa stared at the necklace in awe. It was beautiful, an

onyx pendant with a thin silver chain. 'What do you mean, it will take you to her?'

'My parents collect all kinds of things,' Suleiman said. 'This necklace contains magic that can teleport you to places. But not just anywhere – only to someone who needs help.'

'Wow,' Rumaysa said.

They were silent as the carpet glided ever further upwards, winding its way through the forest canopy.

'Nearly there,' Zabina called after a while. It did seem like the trees were beginning to thin and the moon was getting brighter.

'I can't wait to get to bed,' Suleiman said, stifling a yawn.

'Duck!' Zabina hissed.

Rumaysa flattened herself on the carpet. 'Duck!' she hissed, but it was too late.

'Whoa!' Suleiman cried, swerving on the carpet as they passed beneath a low-hanging branch. 'Ow!' he exclaimed as a thorn scraped his back.

'No!' Zabina gasped.

Rumaysa looked round in alarm as suddenly the trees around them seemed to twitch. Then, slowly, they began to straighten, rising from their slumber. In the far distance, a menacing growl echoed through the woods.

Rumaysa froze. She knew that sound.

'The Witch knows,' Rumaysa whispered, fear gripping her.

'We need to move!' Zabina said. 'Hurry!'

Rumaysa felt sick. 'The Witch is coming, Suleiman! We need to get out of the forest, *now.*'

Suleiman's eyes widened with terror as he urged the carpet up. Far below, the ground began to shake. The trees raised their branches and began to merge together over their heads.

'Hold on!' Suleiman cried, just as the flying carpet gave a kick and moved even faster upwards, desperately trying to get over the trees. Rumaysa gasped at the speed, the wind whipping at their faces with its deadly chill. But more and more thorny branches shot up, reaching high into the sky. Rumaysa whirled in every direction, but there was now a thick, impenetrable canopy above. Not even a glimpse of moonlight could break through.

She gasped. 'Oh no!' Her heart began to race, thudding harder and harder against her chest.

They were trapped.

'We need to get out of here,' Rumaysa said desperately, trying to breathe deeply through her panic. Her head was

starting to ring. 'We can't go over, so we need to go through. But the river . . .'

'What about the river?' Suleiman asked worriedly.

'It's poisonous – I don't know how we'll make it past there.'

'I flew over it – I'm sure we can fly over it again,' Suleiman said. 'But it's so dark – how will we find our way there?' he added desperately as the carpet slowed, unable to see which way to go in the pitch black.

Rumaysa had to think fast. She closed her eyes in concentration. If they no longer had light from the moon, they needed light from somewhere else. But *what* . . . ?

Her eyes flew open as she remembered the other night in her tower.

The magic inside Rumaysa felt like a small light that waited for her call to bring it out. She wrapped herself around it and began to hum. The melody felt like lakes and sunshine, but she couldn't keep her voice steady. The violent rustling around them from the trees and the thought of Cordelia coming was enough to make her feel faint.

'What's going on?' Suleiman cried fearfully. The carpet dived to avoid a snaking branch reaching for them.

Everyone screamed.

'Focus, Rumaysa,' Zabina said in a calming voice.

Rumaysa forced herself to take deep, comforting breaths and turned her thoughts inwards. She hummed, and, as she did so, her magic began to flow out of her. Slowly, tiny lights began to flicker in front of them.

'Fireflies!' Suleiman gasped.

Rumaysa continued her tune as more fireflies appeared, lighting the way for them.

As the carpet swooped through the trees, she kept her eyes closed, silently imploring the tiny creatures to show them the way. Next to her, Zabina and Suleiman were listening out for any noises, looking over their shoulders in terror.

A hair-raising cackle boomed over the woods as another branch came flying at them. Everybody ducked as the carpet soared upwards, narrowly avoiding the tips of the thorny branches trying to ensnare them.

'It's too dangerous on the carpet!' Zabina shouted.

'We're almost there! I can hear the river!' Rumaysa cried.

But as the sounds of gushing water came closer to them, a new cold seemed to take over. Rumaysa could see her breath before her. The hairs on the back of her neck stood up.

'Just a bit further!' Zabina said fearfully.

'Hurry!' Rumaysa shouted at Suleiman.

'I'm trying!' Suleiman squeaked.

He urged the carpet on, and Rumaysa prayed desperately that they would make it. She could see a break in the trees ahead of them that she hoped would lead them to the river.

But before they could break free of the woods, a loud rumbling erupted around them. The entire forest began to shake, more violently than before, and a terrible thunder echoed through the woods. The earth beneath them cracked and a large branch swung out of nowhere, knocking Rumaysa and Suleiman off the carpet.

Rumaysa screamed as she tumbled through the air, landing with a hard crash on the frozen ground. She scrambled to her feet as fast as she could. 'Zabina! Suleiman!'

Suleiman groaned in response. He was lying on the ground, but there was no sign of his carpet. Zabina was perched on his head looking ruffled. 'I'm here, Rumaysa!'

Rumaysa rushed over to them, her heart hammering.

'ROMSARA!' Cordelia's scream seemed to come from all around them. There was a rush of wind above their heads.

Suleiman scrabbled to his feet as Zabina sprang into the air, and the three of them sped towards an opening ahead where the trees began to thin out. The sound of water became louder.

'You think you can escape from me, do you?' Cordelia's iron voice growled.

Suleiman and Rumaysa skidded to a halt in the middle of the clearing. Cordelia was standing at the edge of the thick, bubbling river, her black cloak billowing behind her in the wind. The children looked frantically about their surroundings. There was no way across.

'I commend you, Romeesa – you made it this far,' the Witch sneered, slowly stalking forward.

'L-leave us be, Witch!' Suleiman stammered, hesitantly pulling a dagger from his pocket.

Cordelia's head turned towards Suleiman. 'Who are you, boy?' she snarled. 'How did you come upon the girl?'

Suleiman looked petrified. 'I-I was travelling and saw the tower—'

'This boy is trying to steal you for his own use,' Cordelia interrupted, speaking to Rumaysa in a poisonous voice. 'Did you really think you could trust a stranger? Haven't I been telling you for years, Rumaysa, that I'm the only one you can trust?'

Rumaysa wanted to tell Cordelia that Suleiman had not been part of her plan, but she was lost for words. She desperately looked around her for an exit, but the only way was back into the forest – or forward, towards the Witch.

Cordelia laughed, her blood-red lips stretching wide. 'The outside world is no place for a girl like you,' she crooned. 'You know you don't belong here. I can keep you safe.'

'I'll never go back!' Rumaysa said fiercely, finding her voice. Her hands were shaking.

'Come with me now and I'll forgive you,' Cordelia said silkily. 'I can make you strong and powerful, teach you how to use that magic of yours. We're going to live in our golden palace, remember?'

'W-what do you mean, teach me how to use my magic?' Rumaysa said, her voice trembling. She curled her quaking hands into fists.

'You can feel it, can't you?' Cordelia hissed.

Rumaysa's whole body was shaking now. She could feel her magic pulsing through her as her anger grew. It felt as though it were trying to push out of her skin.

'Rumaysa, don't listen to her!' yelled Suleiman. He lunged

at the Witch, but with one snap of her fingers his dagger turned into a thick branch that reared up and threw itself towards him, striking him over the head.

Suleiman collapsed to the ground. Zabina dived down towards him, but another sharp branch came flying at her, forcing her to swoop upwards to avoid its spiky edges.

'No!' Rumaysa shouted as the branch rose threateningly once more. Her hand instinctively flew out and, with a shock of energy that crackled through her skin, a beam of golden light shot from it. There was a flash and the branch froze where it was, poised to strike.

Rumaysa stared at her hand in awe.

Anger flickered across Cordelia's cool mask. 'How dare you defy me? You think you can just run off with some fool and live happily ever after, just because he rescued you?'

Rumaysa bristled. 'I'm not running off with him! *He* didn't rescue me. I escaped by *myself*!'

'You? Escaped by yourself?' Cordelia sneered.

Rumaysa quaked with anger.

The Witch cackled, her mouth widening into a snarling grin. 'You want your freedom, Romsara? You think you can just walk back into your homeland? You'll never be accepted; you're a witch's child!'

'I am not your child!' Rumaysa shouted.

Cordelia laughed cruelly at her. 'Well, your real parents aren't around, are they? All this time you've been locked away, and they've never even tried to find you.'

'Don't listen to her!' Zabina shouted.

'Ah, the wretched owl!' Cordelia hissed as Zabina swooped above them. She curled her fingers menacingly and a ball of red light appeared in her palm.

'Fly, Zabina!' Rumaysa screamed, realizing what the Witch was about to do.

Zabina took flight, diving behind a tree as Cordelia threw the fiery light at her. The branch shielding her was singed away into ash. Cordelia threw another raging ball at the owl, and this time it struck its target. Zabina yelped, falling to the ground unconscious.

'*Zabina!*' Rumaysa cried in horror.

Cordelia snarled. 'Enough of this foolishness. I'm taking you to our new home and you will *never* be able to leave it, Romeesa!'

Rumaysa stared from Zabina's unconscious form to Suleiman's. Anger rose viciously in her body, energy burning under her skin. She couldn't go back to the tower, not after all of this.

The magic rushed through her veins, demanding to be let out. Her hands flew forward and golden beams came streaming out, hitting Cordelia square in the chest. 'MY. NAME. IS. RUMAYSA!' she roared.

The Witch shouted in surprise as she was sent flying backwards. She landed with a loud splash in the thick, green water.

'Rumaysa, help me! Throw me your hijab! Give me a rope!' Cordelia screamed as the water around her began to bubble. She shrieked, flapping her arms above her head. 'Wasn't I kind to you?'

'You used me!' Rumaysa shouted.

'I promise I won't hurt you again!' Cordelia pleaded. 'Just get me out! Please, help me!'

Rumaysa lurched forward, as if to help Cordelia, but a great wave rose up and lapped over the Witch.

'Rumaysa!' Cordelia roared as the water rose once more around her. Rumaysa had to look away as she disappeared into bubbling froth.

Eventually, her screaming stopped.

The water stilled.

'Cordelia?' Rumaysa said uncertainly.

The waters did not move, nor did Cordelia reply.

Rumaysa's knees gave way. She crumpled to the ground, staring at the spot where the Witch had disappeared.

She couldn't believe what she had done. Cordelia was gone.

Rumaysa couldn't bear to look at the water any longer. She struggled up and hurried to Zabina. She gently shook her small body, hoping and praying that she would wake up. For one frightening moment, it seemed as if she wouldn't.

'Ow,' Zabina groaned.

'Oh, Zabina!' Rumaysa cried in relief. She pulled her friend into a feathery hug.

Suleiman stirred. 'My head really hurts,' he grumbled, clambering slowly to his feet.

Zabina blinked blearily at Rumaysa. 'Where's Cordelia?'

Rumaysa looked back at the river. 'She's gone,' she said quietly.

Zabina's eyes widened. 'Really?'

Rumaysa nodded.

Suddenly, the earth began to shake again. The trio

gathered together, staring around in fright as the trees behind them quaked. For one wild moment, Rumaysa thought that they were about to be attacked again. But instead of reaching towards them, the trees began to crash into the ground, shrinking before their very eyes.

'What's happening?' Suleiman gasped in awe.

'Cordelia's gone. Her forest must be going too,' Rumaysa said, watching in shock as the thick, dark trees that had encased her for her whole life shrivelled into the ground.

'Let's get out of here,' Zabina squawked.

Rumaysa sighed with relief. 'Yes, let's.'

Suleiman looked at them both blankly.

'Let's get out of here,' Rumaysa explained.

'Oh! Yes, please!' he said. Then he gave a long, loud whistle.

All was quiet for a moment, and then a familiar whooshing sound hit the air. The battered carpet came hurtling out of the falling trees, stopping gracefully in front of them.

The three of them climbed on and the rug launched across the river.

'Is the Witch gone for good?' Suleiman asked.

'She must be,' Rumaysa replied. She looked back, stunned to see the forest had all but disappeared. Far away in the distance, she could see her tower standing tall amid the barren ground.

When they landed on the other side of the river, the group hoorayed and cheered as they practically fell with relief on to the safe, snowy grass.

'We actually did it,' Rumaysa breathed, looking in awe around her.

Endless grass stretched out beyond them, and in the distance they could see snow-covered hills and tiny flickering lights. Not one spiky tree was in sight.

'I can't believe she's really gone,' Rumaysa said again.

'You have your whole life ahead of you now!' Zabina said excitedly. 'Will you go and find your parents?'

'I don't know,' Rumaysa said. 'I wouldn't know how to find them . . .'

'Find who?' Suleiman asked.

'My parents,' Rumaysa explained.

'I think my necklace could help you. Here,' he said, handing it to her with a smile.

Rumaysa took it from him uncertainly. 'Are you sure?'

'You need it more than I do. Besides, I have my magic carpet.'

Feeling touched, Rumaysa smiled weakly back. She peered at the necklace. 'How does it work?'

'Well, I'm not entirely sure,' he said, his dark brows furrowing. 'I guess if you think of the person you want to see most, it should start to glow.'

'I thought you said it keeps bringing you to the wrong people?' Rumaysa said.

Suleiman's face reddened. 'I guess I might have been doing something wrong. But you can find your parents with it – I'm sure,' he continued earnestly. 'Just think long and hard about who you want to see.'

'Well, thank you,' Rumaysa said.

Suleiman nodded and smiled, settling back on his magic carpet. 'I wish I could go back home, but I'd better carry on looking for the Princess . . .' He sighed. 'Good luck, Rumaysa. Thank you for saving me from that witch. And you too, owl!'

Zabina hooted back. 'Goodbye, boy!'

Suleiman waved as his carpet rose again, and Rumaysa watched as he flew off, disappearing into the horizon.

Eventually, she turned to Zabina. For a moment, the girl and the owl just stared at each other sadly.

'I don't know how to ever thank you, Zabina, for everything,' Rumaysa said, tears filling her eyes again. 'I probably would have lost my mind in there if it wasn't for you.'

Zabina's wide blue eyes were watery too. 'Don't thank me, Rumaysa. It's been my greatest gift, to have you as my best friend.'

Rumaysa's face crumpled. She gathered Zabina in a hug as they both failed to hold back their tears.

'Now is your time to go and have adventures,' Zabina said, drawing back with a great sniff.

'Why don't you come with me?' Rumaysa offered, wiping her runny nose with the back of her hand.

'I could . . . but I have a date with the raven on Saturday!' Zabina said, ruffling her feathers with excitement.

Rumaysa burst out laughing. 'Now's the time for you to live your own life, as well, Zabina. You've spent long enough looking after me.'

'I'd do it all over again, Rumaysa, believe me,' Zabina said.

They hugged again.

'Go on – you need to find your parents!' Zabina said, flapping at Rumaysa. 'Come and visit me, though, won't you?'

'I promise,' Rumaysa said, nodding.

Zabina smiled and hopped back.

Rumaysa clasped her hand round the onyx necklace and closed her eyes. She had no idea what her parents looked like, but she thought of the two people that had brought her into this world. Her missing family. *Take me to my parents. Please take me to my parents.*

A strange pulse emanated from the necklace in Rumaysa's hand. Her eyes flew open as a wind gathered around her. Rumaysa just caught the surprised look on Zabina's feathery face when the world began to spin and the ground beneath her feet opened up, whirling her away into purple smoke.

Rumaysa had no idea where she was going or what she would find, but she knew she was ready to face whatever would come her way.

Cinderayla

I

Once upon a time, in a land not far from Splinterfell, a young girl lived with her parents in a beautiful manor house in the glittering city of Qamaroon. Of all the children in Qamaroon, none could say they were as happy as young Ayla. She lived with her mother, a wise woman who curated artwork, and her father, a tradesman.

Ayla spent many days with her mother, either painting in the garden or in the village park, where her mother found inspiration from the townspeople. Ayla took after her mother in many ways. They had the same curly brown hair, the same warm-brown skin and hazel eyes. The only thing she'd inherited from her father was his height.

All sorts of people came by their house to see her mother's

work, and some came just to talk to her. There are few people on this earth who are simply kind and sincere. Tahira was such a person. Ayla watched her mother bring comfort to countless people, either through a smile or sage advice. If you were ever to ask Ayla what she wanted to be when she grew up, she would readily say her mother.

Ayla and Tahira would often walk home together under the evening sun and arrive to find Ayla's father with dinner on the table. Adam was a fantastic cook and loved to experiment with new recipes when he got the chance.

Evenings often passed with new dishes and games until Ayla became tired, when both parents would tuck her in and bid her goodnight. As much as she hated to go to sleep, Ayla couldn't wait to begin the day again with her little family.

As fate would have it, though, not all would stay well in their household. One morning, Ayla found she wasn't able to spend the day with her mother, for Tahira was feeling unwell. Ayla hoped she'd feel well enough to go to the park the next day, but as the days turned into weeks Tahira still didn't get any better. Before long, Tahira could barely get out of bed.

Ayla made sure to bring all the fun to her parents' room, trying to put a smile on her mother's face and take the worry lines off her father's. Tahira watched her daughter with the biggest smile she could muster, trying to hide her coughs and weakness from her. Adam did all he could to find a cure for her sickness, but it seemed no doctor in Qamaroon could help. Time, they said. Make the most of it, whatever was left.

Losing a loved one is a strange thing. It can come upon you out of nowhere, knocking you sideways and changing the colour of your life for many years to come. When Tahira breathed her last, there was nothing but stillness in the house. Shock lingered for days, until Adam realized he had to make preparations, and Ayla realized her mother would never come back.

Time passed, but their grief lingered. Ayla grew into a smart, compassionate young girl, while Adam grew wealthier and lonelier. He did his best for his daughter, trying to help her paint as often as he could and teaching her how to cook. Ayla cherished her time with her father and was grateful for his company.

Adam was a gentle man, and a good father, but Ayla knew he was lonely. And, it just so happened that Adam met a beautiful noble lady on one of his trips with the trading caravans.

'Ayla,' Adam began at breakfast one morning, 'I have something to tell you.'

'Yes, Abbu?' she said.

'I know it's just been me and you for a while, since . . . since . . .' He looked away briefly, tears brimming in his brown eyes. 'Since your mother passed.' It never got easier to say. 'She made me promise that one day I would move on, when the time was right.'

Ayla looked at him in surprise. 'Really?'

'Yes, dear. Your mother was an especially thoughtful woman.' He still spoke of her with so much love.

'So . . .' Ayla prompted, a strange knot forming in her stomach.

Her father looked at her again. 'I feel that time is now.'

Ayla wasn't sure what to say.

'She's a lovely woman, very intelligent. She lost her husband a few years ago. And she has two daughters who are the same age as you, so you'll have sisters to play with. Won't that be lovely?'

'Sisters?' Ayla repeated excitedly, the knot loosening. 'That would be wonderful!'

The next evening, Ayla watched happily from her bedroom

window as a brown carriage pulled by two black stallions came trundling down their road.

Her soon-to-be stepmother climbed out. She was a tall woman with brown skin and high cheekbones. She wore a dark purple gown with matching lipstick and carried an air of importance about her. Behind her came her daughters.

Ayla ran down the stairs to the entrance hall.

'Amelia, this is my daughter, Ayla,' Adam said.

Ayla beamed up at Amelia.

'Hello, dear!' Amelia said in a kind voice. 'My, my, aren't you a beautiful little girl!'

'Pleased to meet you!' Ayla said, curtseying.

'These are Rubina and Sufina,' Amelia said, pulling her daughters forward.

Rubina and Sufina were twins, born just a minute apart, but they were not identical. Rubina had wild curly hair, and Sufina had short straight hair. Rubina was also a bit taller, and Sufina's face was rounder.

The introductions over, everybody sat down to dinner.

'Oh, this looks absolutely wonderful, darling!' Amelia said to Ayla's father.

'Ayla helped me,' Adam said graciously.

'How splendid – you must be an excellent cook, Ayla!' Amelia said.

'She is, indeed,' Adam replied proudly.

'Well, I can't *wait* to try more of your food,' she said, smiling widely at Ayla.

Ayla smiled back, happy that Amelia seemed so impressed with her.

'Girls, what do we say?' Amelia said in a quieter voice to her daughters.

'Thank you,' Rubina and Sufina chorused.

Amelia looked around the room discreetly over the top of her water glass. 'You have such a wonderful home, Adam. We'll be one big happy family here.'

The wedding ceremony followed soon after, and all seemed well in Ayla's house. Although she still missed her mother terribly, her father always made sure to spend time with her, taking her to the park or anywhere else she wanted to go. Ayla thought she might have imagined it, but she sensed an air of disapproval from Amelia whenever this happened.

Amelia took to her new household with vigour. She had a very specific way of doing things and a particular style. She put up new wallpaper, new curtains and new – well, everything. Adam didn't want to change the household furniture, things his Tahira had picked out, but he didn't want Amelia to be unhappy either, and he knew it was important for her to feel comfortable in her new home.

Ayla tried to save as much of the house as possible, taking anything she could into the attic. She sensed a hostility from Amelia sometimes, but didn't know how to voice it to her father. Perhaps Amelia was just getting used to having a new family, and Ayla could see how much Amelia and her father loved each other. All she wanted was for her father to be happy.

Rubina and Sufina seemed to like Ayla, at least. Sometimes the three played dress-up or made different baked goods. Amelia always seemed to praise her own daughters more, though, delighting in all they did with exaggerated fervour.

A year after Adam and Amelia's wedding, Ayla's father was preparing to take his next business trip. Amelia and the girls all lined up to say goodbye to him as the carriages arrived.

'Now, Ayla,' he said to her, 'I want you to look after everybody while I am away, OK?'

Ayla nodded glumly. 'Do you have to go, Father? Can't you just miss this one trip?'

Adam felt a great sadness saying goodbye to his daughter; he hated to leave Ayla behind. 'I'm afraid so, sweetheart,' he said.

'Can't I come with you?' she asked hopefully.

'I'm sorry, Ayla – it wouldn't be safe to take you,' her father said.

Ayla tried to hold back her tears. 'Hurry home, please. I'll miss you.'

'I'll do my best,' he said, giving her a warm hug before he departed. 'I'll miss you too, my darling girl.'

Ayla didn't know it would be the last time she would see her beloved father. While on board a ship travelling to a neighbouring land, a deadly storm caught his vessel at night. When the news reached Ayla and her stepfamily, she was sure her heart would break and break until there was nothing left.

Amelia was beside herself. She was now twice widowed with another daughter to look after.

'How could he leave me?' Amelia wailed from her room. 'My life is ruined!'

Amelia wept for days and days as Ayla stayed in her own bedroom, crying silently by herself.

Eventually, the grief that gripped Ayla's household began to wane. Ayla left her room and found herself doing odd chores around the house to help pass the time. She cooked every day, trying to recreate her father's recipes. It made her feel less far away from him.

'Ayla, would you be a dear and get me tea, please?' Amelia began to ask.

'Ayla, can you iron my clothes?' Rubina requested.

'Ayla, can you mend my socks?' Sufina asked.

At first, Ayla welcomed the distraction of her stepfamily's requests. They were mundane but frequent, and Ayla found it took her mind off everything else.

But things began to take a turn. Soon, they stopped asking and started demanding.

'Ayla, get my lunch!' Amelia snapped.

'Ayla, where is my schoolwork?' Sufina shrieked.

'Give Sufina your room – my girls are too big to share now. You can sleep in the attic,' Amelia decided one night, all but throwing Ayla out of her bedroom.

It seemed like Ayla was being pushed further and further out of her own home.

There are often tipping points in life, and here was another one for our young heroine. She soon began to understand her new place. Now that her father was gone, Amelia ran the household. Rubina and Sufina became as insufferable as their mother, ordering Ayla to do this and that with no regard for her own feelings or needs. Twelve miserable months had passed since her father's death. She was a servant in her own home.

*

Ayla woke one morning to the sound of the royal bells. She got up from her old wooden bed and opened her attic window to see the commotion. The people of Qamaroon were rushing out of their homes excitedly. Several guards on horseback were coming down the road, dressed in Qamaroon's national colours of silver and navy. The guard at the forefront of the procession was ringing a bell wildly, shouting, 'Attention, all loyal subjects! This is your royal guard! We have an announcement from the King!'

The people outside were silent in anticipation.

'By order of the Prince of Qamaroon, every maiden in the land is invited to attend the royal Eid ball one week from today at the palace!'

This announcement was met with gasps of delight, and cheers erupted in the street. After the month of fasting in Ramadan, the King usually had a ball, but it was mostly for other royals and the aristocracy. This was the first time that ordinary citizens would get to attend.

Ayla had never been to so much as a town festival, let alone an Eid ball. She wondered if Amelia would let her go.

The sound of delighted screaming reached Ayla in her attic. She tiptoed over to her door and walked out to the oak banister, leaning over so she could hear the conversation downstairs.

'What shall we wear?' Rubina squealed.

'Mama, I need a new dress, please!' Sufina whined.

'A ball!' Amelia shrieked. 'With any luck, I'll find husbands for you both!'

Ayla sighed. She knew she was going to be made to help them all prepare for the ball. And, as she turned back to her room, Amelia called her name.

'Ayla, get down here!

Ayla slowly headed down the attic stairs, each step creaking as she descended three floors to the parlour. It was chaos. Rubina and Sufina were lost amid a pile of dresses. Amelia was pacing the floor, excitement clear on her otherwise sour face.

'Ayla, take these fabrics at once to Mrs Khan in the market and get them tailored to fit the girls,' Amelia barked, throwing a pile of materials at her. 'And get them shoes from Zaza's and jewellery to match!' she added, tossing a pouch of coins on top of the cloth in Ayla's hands.

'All the maidens of the land are invited to the Eid ball!' Sufina said excitedly, dancing around Ayla. 'I shall find the Prince and make him fall in love with me!'

'No, I'll make him fall in love with *me*!' Rubina said

indignantly, shoving into Sufina. 'I'm older than you, so I get to have him!'

'You're only older by one minute!' Sufina said angrily, shoving her back. 'I'm smarter! Who'd want *you* for a wife?'

'Aren't you a bit young to get married?' Ayla mumbled under her breath.

'Take that back!' Rubina shrieked, lunging at Sufina.

'Girls, stop it,' Amelia said distractedly, inspecting herself in the mirror. She caught sight of her stepdaughter in the reflection. 'Ayla, go now!' she barked.

Ayla hurried out of the room.

'Perhaps I can find a husband for myself, too,' she heard Amelia muse to herself.

Ayla's eyes widened. Amelia had barely stopped crying a few weeks ago!

Ayla grabbed a large cloak to cover her worn clothes. She put the fabrics neatly in a string bag and headed out eagerly to the town. Spring was upon Qamaroon; the ground was slowly losing its frost and the fresh air had a warmer bite to it that Ayla welcomed.

She headed to Mrs Khan's house, a few roads away from her own, to deliver the fabrics for tailoring. She gave the girls'

92

measurements and left, thinking she'd drop by the market on her way home.

The market was full of different stalls selling food, clothes, bric-á-brac and all sorts. Hints of chocolate and syrup from the sweets stall wafted in the air, tinged with the smell of savoury goods frying from the hot-food stands. Ayla marvelled at the sight and sounds of all the townspeople hurrying about.

'Coin a bowl!' the fruit man was yelling. 'Coin a bowl! Get your fruits 'ere, fresh from the farm! Coin a bowl!'

Ayla remembered coming to the market sometimes with her parents. They used to let her pick one treat on her way home. She headed for the sweets stall and ordered one jalebi from the woman behind the counter. It was two silver coins, so hopefully Amelia wouldn't notice. Ayla ate her sweet treat quickly, before heading off to finish her errands.

When she returned to the manor, feeling energized for once, Ayla took a look through her mother's clothes. She found a beautiful pink silk dress with gold embroidery all over it. It didn't quite fit, but all the mending and stitching of her stepfamily's clothes meant that she was now very handy with a needle. Ayla began the alterations, excitement coursing through her. Amelia hadn't said that she *couldn't* go, and that was good enough for Ayla!

III

The next day, Ayla was once again summoned to help her stepsisters prepare for the ball. Rubina and Sufina were a bubble of excitement as Ayla made their fresh face masks and helped comb out their hair. She had to try different styles on them, even though the ball was still six days away.

While Ayla was attempting to tie up Rubina's unruly hair in an intricate plait, Sufina asked dreamily, 'What are you going to wear, Ayla?'

'Oh, I-I'm not sure,' Ayla said, eyes darting nervously to her stepmother, who was sitting in the corner.

'What do you mean?' Amelia said slowly, looking at Ayla. 'You can't possibly think you're invited?'

'But I thought the royal guard said all the maidens in the land, Mother,' Sufina said.

'Yes, but Ayla can't go!' Amelia scoffed. 'I've had enough hardship paying for your two dresses as it is. Besides, her clothes are patched; her face is a mess. No father *or* mother to present her! No, it just wouldn't do!'

Ayla felt her face going red. 'I-I have something of my mother's I could wear. It wouldn't cost you anything.' She spoke quietly. She didn't want to anger Amelia.

Amelia snorted. 'I'm doing you a favour, Ayla, trust me. If you turn up in your old rags, everybody will simply laugh at you. You wouldn't want to be humiliated, would you?'

'Mother, why don't you let her come as our maid, then?' Sufina suggested. 'She can help carry our things and fetch us drinks. It'll make us look like we're rich!'

Amelia considered the idea. 'Well, that's a point. But you are not to talk or speak to anyone else, and you must stay with me at all times – do you hear, Ayla?'

Ayla fought to keep the smile off her face. 'Yes, Amelia. Thank you.'

Sufina caught Ayla's eye and gave her a tentative smile.

*

On the morning of the Eid ball, the city of Qamaroon was abuzz with anticipation. Ayla went to collect her stepsisters' dresses, and when she returned home Rubina and Sufina practically tore them from her hands, such was their excitement.

'Ayla, you need to iron my dress,' Rubina demanded with a huff.

'You need to help with my hair!' Sufina said.

'No, she's helping me!' Rubina growled.

'Girls, do shut up!' Amelia yelled from her bedroom.

'I can help you both,' Ayla said, smiling despite herself. 'Come, let's get ready.'

Ayla spent the whole day helping the girls prepare. Rubina wanted a mountain of curls piled on top of her head; Sufina wanted an elegant bun that required more pins than Ayla could count. The whole morning and afternoon went in a blur as Ayla worked hard to make her stepsisters wishes come to reality.

'Oh, you did such a wonderful job on my hair!' Rubina gasped as she took sight of her curls in the mirror.

'Wow,' Sufina breathed, admiring her reflection as she stood next to her sister.

Ayla smiled, genuinely happy to have helped.

She left her stepsisters and ran up to her attic to put her dress on. She'd spent every night of the past week sewing it to fit and it slipped on like a glove.

Its bell sleeves and skirt flared out, making Ayla feel like a princess. She wrapped her dupatta on neatly and pinned it with a gold brooch that had belonged to her mother. Her mother's shoes were unfortunately too big for her, so she had to wear her tatty black slippers. But her dress pretty much covered them anyway.

Ayla looked at herself in the mirror. Grief had long since stripped her face of its glow, but her brown eyes were bright. She felt something close to happiness for the first time in a while. She could see her mother in her own reflection; her warm face smiling, brown curls cascading down her back. Ayla wished she were here to help her get ready for her first ball.

At six, the carriages arrived. Ayla could hear the girls squabbling over who looked better as she nervously went downstairs. When she descended into the hallway, her stepfamily froze at the sight of her.

'Wow,' Sufina and Rubina said at the same time.

Amelia gaped for a moment, but quickly rearranged her features. 'What on earth are you wearing?' she scoffed.

'It's an old dress of my mother's,' Ayla said uncertainly.

'It's hideous – you can't wear that to the ball!' Amelia sneered.

'It's a nice dress, Mother – what do you mean?' Rubina asked confusedly.

'Be quiet,' Amelia hissed at her. She marched over to Ayla. 'What is this tatty old dress?' She grabbed Ayla's arm with one hand and her sleeve with the other. 'It's so out of date!' Ayla tried to back away from her, but as she did Amelia put her foot down on the hem of the dress.

There was a loud tearing sound as the skirt of Ayla's dress split apart from the bodice.

Ayla gasped. 'What are you doing?'

'Oh dear – it's ripped,' Amelia said coldly. 'The whole thing is practically falling apart!'

'Mother, what are you doing?' Sufina said in a small voice.

'You shall not go to the ball!' Amelia shouted, now tearing Ayla's sleeve from the dress.

'Stop it! Leave me alone!' Ayla sobbed.

'Mother, we have to go – we're going to be late,' Sufina said, dragging Amelia away. She didn't dare look directly at Ayla.

'Let's go, Mother,' Rubina said in a shocked voice, helping to pull her towards the door.

'Get back to your chores!' Amelia said contemptuously,

casting Ayla an angry glare before disappearing out of the door with her daughters.

Ayla stood in the hallway by herself, sobbing. Her mother's beautiful dress was destroyed.

As much as she loved her father, Ayla hated him in that moment. She hated him for going on that fateful trip and leaving her without him, for leaving her with her cruel stepmother..

She rushed outside, crying, unable to be in the house any longer. She could see her stepfamily's carriage disappearing down the lane. She picked up a rock from the ground and threw it with all her might in their direction. She threw another one and another one, angry tears pouring down her face.

IV

Rumaysa landed with a hard thud on the ground. 'Zabina?' she said. Her owl friend was nowhere to be seen.

She looked around uncertainly. She was on a road of some sort, lined with beautiful big houses.

'Look out, miss!' a man's voice yelled.

Rumaysa jumped back as a carriage came trundling past her, carrying an elegantly dressed woman and two girls inside. She looked around again, unsure where to go.

A stone came flying out of nowhere and landed at her feet. A moment later, another stone followed, and then another one.

This is very rude, Rumaysa thought. First, she almost got run over by a carriage, and now someone was hurling rocks at her. What *was* this place? Why did the necklace bring her here? The only person in need was her – to be saved from the flying stones!

Rumaysa looked ahead and saw a small figure, sobbing as it threw one final rock before it turned, shoulders sagging, and walked off towards one of the houses.

Rumaysa looked at the necklace in her hand. It was glowing a deep purple again. She closed her eyes and wished to find her parents, but when she opened them, she was still in the street.

The necklace gave a tug. Rumaysa raised her eyebrows as she found herself walking as though pulled by a magnetic force.

'Where are you taking me?' she said exasperatedly. It seemed to be leading her towards the place where the rocks had come from.

The glow of the necklace began to fade as its pull lessened. Up ahead, the small figure was now sitting on the doorstep of one of the houses. The necklace went still.

Rumaysa stared at it, then at the figure, and Suleiman's voice rang in her mind: *'This is meant to take me to the princess,*

the one most in need, but I keep ending up in different places with
no sign of her.'

Rumaysa sighed. She had a feeling that, whoever this girl was, she had nothing to do with Rumaysa's parents. Tentatively, she walked closer to the figure that was now sitting with a bowed head making sniffing noises. It was a young girl in a ragged dress.

'Hello?' Rumaysa called into the darkening sunset.

The girl looked up with a start. 'Who are you?'

Rumaysa could see the girl properly now under a tall lantern hanging above the gate. She had brown skin, curly dark hair and sad eyes. Her face was blotched from crying and Rumaysa could see her pink dress was torn. 'My name is Rumaysa. What's yours?'

'Ayla,' the girl replied, wiping her tear-streaked face.

'Are you OK?' Rumaysa asked.

Ayla looked as if she hadn't been asked that in a very long time. 'I don't know.'

'What happened to your dress?' Rumaysa tried again.

Ayla shrugged. 'It got ruined.' Then, clearly trying to change the subject, she said, 'Why are you here, Rumaysa?'

Rumaysa wondered if somebody else had ruined Ayla's

dress. That would explain the rocks at least. 'I'm looking for my parents,' she replied.

Ayla's brown eyes widened again. 'Are they here in Qamaroon?'

'I'm not sure. I've never met them. A witch stole me when I was a baby and held me captive ever since. I just escaped today.'

Ayla looked shocked, and slightly afraid. 'How did you escape?'

'I, er, made an escape rope-scarf from straw and climbed out of the tower,' Rumaysa said sheepishly.

'How did you make a scarf from straw?' Ayla asked, puzzled.

'Oh, well, I can spin straw and make . . . stuff out of it.' She didn't think she should mention her magic at this point. 'I could help you mend your dress?' Rumaysa offered, changing the subject.

Ayla looked sad again. 'No, it's OK. I don't need it any more.'

'What did you need it for in the first place?' Rumaysa asked gently.

Ayla shifted slightly on the step. 'I was going to go to the ball. All the people of Qamaroon are invited, so I thought I could go, but . . .'

'But?' Rumaysa prompted after a moment.

Ayla shrugged, tears pooling in her eyes again. 'My stepmother wouldn't let me.'

Rumaysa was taken aback. 'Why not?'

'I don't know – she's just . . .' Ayla trailed off with a frustrated sigh.

Rumaysa knew the feeling well. 'Why don't you go to the ball anyway?'

The girl shook her head tearfully. 'I can't.'

The necklace suddenly gave a little tug in Rumaysa's hand. 'I think you should go to the ball,' she said.

'I can't – if my stepmother sees me, then I'll be in serious trouble.'

The necklace tugged again, harder. After a moment Rumaysa said, 'What if she can't recognize you?'

Ayla was confused, but there was something about Rumaysa that made her feel that she could trust her. 'Why don't you come in, at least? You must be hungry.'

Rumaysa agreed and followed Ayla into her house. She stared in wonder at the large entry hall and spiral staircase. There were rooms on either side of the hallway decorated in rich emerald and oak colours. After staring at her own grey walls for years, Rumaysa felt like this was what a palace must look like.

Ayla took Rumaysa down the stairs into the kitchen, where she marvelled at the sight of a stove, a large wooden dining table and all the different pots and pans in the room.

'Are you OK?' Ayla asked, noticing Rumaysa looking around in wonder.

'I've just never seen an actual kitchen before,' Rumaysa replied. 'Or a house. Or anything, really.'

Ayla didn't know how to respond. 'You can sit here,' she said after a moment. She gestured to one of the chairs. 'I'll get you some food.'

Rumaysa sat down tentatively. She brushed the top of the table with her finger, feeling the smooth dark wood with curiosity. Ayla put some warm milk, hot bread and soup in front of her.

'Thank you,' Rumaysa breathed, gingerly picking up the cup of milk. After one cautious sip, she gulped it down eagerly, relishing the fresh taste. The bread and creamy vegetable soup were another delight – her escape down the tower and through the forest had left her ravenous.

Ayla watched Rumaysa eat in faint amusement.

When Rumaysa had finished, she said to Ayla, 'Please let me fix your dress. You've been so kind to give me some food, it's the least I can do.'

Ayla looked at her uncertainly. 'I can't go to the ball.'

'What if I just fix your dress, anyway?' Rumaysa offered.

After a moment's hesitation, Ayla said, 'OK. I have some sewing things in my room. Follow me.'

Rumaysa went with Ayla up to her attic room, right at the top of the stairs. She noticed that the decorations and fancy furniture did not reach this part of the house: the door to Ayla's room was plain brown, and the bedroom walls were peeling with greyed wallpaper. There was a *lot* of stuff in there, though. There were chests of drawers, a table with chairs, a chess board and pictures on the wall. Lots of coloured rugs patterned the hard wood floor.

Ayla saw Rumaysa looking around her cramped room. 'These are a lot of my parents' things.'

'Where are your parents?' Rumaysa asked.

'My mother died when I was young, and my father died about a year ago now.'

'Oh, I'm so sorry,' Rumaysa said.

Ayla smiled weakly in reply, then walked over to an

oak drawer and started rummaging inside. Eventually she brandished a sewing kit. 'Here you go,' she said, handing the box to Rumaysa.

Rumaysa set to work; needles and thread were second nature to her. She asked Ayla to stand in the most spacious part of the room so she could work around her.

Rumaysa could feel from the necklace that she needed to help Ayla; she had a strong suspicion that mending the dress was the first step towards this. She began to stitch up the broken pieces, humming a soft tune as she did so.

Her singing sounded like a lullaby and, with a pang of longing, Ayla was reminded of her happy childhood. Then she noticed the thread begin to glow and gasped as her dress started to change before her very eyes.

'How is this possible?' Ayla breathed.

Rumaysa smiled, humming a little louder as the pink dress transformed into a golden gown. It had an intricate bodice with full sleeves and an iridescent skirt that fanned out.

Ayla could have sworn the goldwork on her dress was real – it shimmered beautifully under the candlelight.

'Let's fix your scarf . . .' Rumaysa worked her magic on the dupatta. By the time she'd finished, Ayla was a golden vision.

'Wow!' was all Ayla could say when she saw her reflection in the mirror. 'You're magical? Is that why the Witch stole you?'

'Pretty much,' Rumaysa said with a rueful smile.

'Wow!' Ayla breathed again, her eyes wide with delight.

Rumaysa stood back, admiring her handiwork with a pleased smile. 'Will you go to the ball now?' she asked.

Ayla looked at her reflection, stunned at the transformation. It would be a shame to waste this beautiful dress, but she just couldn't risk Amelia recognizing her. Then, reflected in the mirror, something caught her eye.

Ayla turned and hurried over to a pile on top of one of the drawers full of her mother's trinkets. A glittering golden mask sat atop some bangles. She grabbed it, putting it to her eyes immediately.

Rumaysa looked at her in awe. 'You look so lovely!'

'Let's go to the ball together!' Ayla said excitedly, a new energy bursting through her. 'I have loads of dresses you can wear. Look!' She pulled open a rickety old cupboard. There were piles and piles of dresses, skirts and blouses inside.

Rumaysa had never seen so many clothes before. She looked down. Her dress was tatty and her body was dirty from her forest escapade. 'I don't think I can come. I need a bath,' she said ruefully.

Ayla was undeterred. 'You can have a bath here – come!' She took Rumaysa's hand and pulled her towards the small bathroom housed in the attic.

After she had bathed – in actual hot water; Rumaysa couldn't believe it! – and dried herself, Rumaysa put on a beautiful blue dress of Ayla's mother's. As the dress fell down her body, Rumaysa marvelled at the soft silk against her skin after a lifetime of scratchy dresses. Ayla had even provided a pale silver scarf. She'd never worn such fine clothes; she felt so overwhelmed by Ayla's kindness.

'You look so wonderful!' Ayla said delightedly as Rumaysa emerged from the bathroom.

The two girls smiled sheepishly at each other. Even though they'd only known one another for a short time, they both felt like they'd been friends for much longer.

Kindred spirits, Ayla's mother would have said. There were some people you just clicked with.

'Thank you, for all of this,' Rumaysa said earnestly. Then she gave a mischievous smile. 'Shall we get going to the ball, then?'

'Yes!' Ayla said excitedly.

They headed out together, hurrying towards the market as Ayla led the way. Eventually they reached the carriage-hire service, where a large sign by a horse stable read:

CUBER
RIDES FOR AS LITTLE AS TWO GOLD COINS

As they got into the carriage, Rumaysa caught sight of Ayla's shoes.

'Are those your shoes for the ball?' Rumaysa asked as they sat down.

Ayla lifted her skirts to reveal the black slippers. 'I don't have anything else,' she said, blushing a little.

'Maybe I can help,' Rumaysa said, looking thoughtfully at the shoes.

While the rider was preparing himself outside the carriage, Rumaysa placed her hands on the slippers. She instinctively knew what she had to do.

The light within Rumaysa pulsed out of her, quickly streaming from her hands. Just a few moments later, Ayla had two golden-heeled shoes on her feet.

'I can't wear *gold* shoes,' Ayla said, staring at them in awe.

'Why not?' Rumaysa asked nervously. 'Are they ugly?' Of course, she didn't know anything about shoes, or what looked the best. Perhaps she should have asked Ayla what she liked.

Ayla shook her head. 'They're beautiful. And so comfortable!'

A huge smile spread across Rumaysa's face. She had the sense that, after all her years of spinning straw, she'd finally made something worthwhile. It felt nice to do something useful for someone who really needed it. She felt the necklace pulse faintly in response round her neck, as if it could hear her thoughts.

V

'Off we go, girls!' the driver said, urging the horses forward. Rumaysa gripped her seat as the carriage took off, trundling away towards the palace.

'How do you do that?' Ayla asked in a quiet voice after a while. 'Turn things into gold?'

'I'm not entirely sure – it just happens,' Rumaysa admitted, still holding tightly to her seat.

'Your parents must be magical too, right?' Ayla asked.

'I have no idea,' Rumaysa said, though she wondered now if that might be the case. 'I don't know anything about them.'

Ayla looked at Rumaysa. 'I'm sorry – that's awful. I'm lucky I got to spend a few years with mine, at least. I can't imagine how you feel.'

Rumaysa wasn't sure how she felt either. It was one thing to grieve a loss, but another thing to grieve something you could only imagine.

They sat in companionable silence until the driver shouted, 'Almost at the palace!'

'Look!' Ayla said excitedly.

A grand white palace came into view, set right on the edge of a cliff that looked out to the ocean. The white stone rose into golden minarets and spires.

'It's so beautiful.' Rumaysa had never seen anything like it.

The sounds of chatter and laughter reached them as the driver pulled up to the gates.

Ayla put her mask on, feeling empowered as she tied the golden ribbons together to hold it in place. She could be anyone here tonight; she didn't have to be a servant, or an orphan. She could be free.

The girls made their way into the palace grounds, where a stage had been set up against the backdrop of the ocean. A canopy of white wisteria hung down in a wicker arch above two golden thrones.

'That's the King!' Ayla said in hushed tones.

Rumaysa looked ahead and saw a tall, rounded man with

dark brown skin and a beaming smile. He wore magnificent navy robes and a golden crown on his head. Something about the King's friendly smile made Rumaysa feel sad, as she wondered what her father might have looked like.

Ayla, in contrast, was immediately mesmerized by the festivities. It was like a dream come true to be at the ball. She couldn't believe her luck as her gold dress glistened under the starlight. Small fireflies hung in the air, like tiny golden stars floating above their heads. The crowd was huge, spilling into the large palace grounds, all dressed in colourful clothes.

The smell of food was intoxicating; Ayla looked around and saw stalls lining the edges of the lawns. There were all kinds of food, from sweet treats like date cakes and creamy kheer, to spicy samosas and lentil fritters. Ayla's stomach rumbled.

'Want to get some food?' she asked Rumaysa.

Rumaysa nodded, grateful to move towards the side. She had never seen so many people before and she was finding it quite overwhelming. The noise of the chatter and music felt alien to her after years of quiet solitude.

'Are you OK?' Ayla asked, sensing Rumaysa's discomfort. 'Here, have some chai.'

Rumaysa took a cup from her and peered into its contents.

It held a creamy brown liquid that smelt like cinnamon and spice. She took a sip. 'This is nice!' she said with surprise.

Ayla grinned. 'Here, try a handesh – it's made from dates.'

She passed her friend a small brown fried pastry. Rumaysa caught its sweet, doughy smell before she gratefully took a bite. It definitely beat oats.

'Come along, girls!' a shrill voice suddenly rang in the air.

Ayla froze. Rumaysa turned and saw a tall woman dressed in a dark gown with a sour, pointy face marching over to the food stalls. She was followed by two girls in puffy red and emerald dresses, both looking around excitedly. Ayla turned away as they neared.

'Is that your stepfamily?' Rumaysa asked quietly.

Ayla nodded. 'Let's head back to the stage.'

As they wended their way through the crowd, heads kept turning to look at Ayla's dress. It shimmered as she walked, the gold glinting as though it might burst into golden flames.

The music slowed and finally stopped, causing the chattering to come to a halt. Everybody turned to look at the King. He was a burly sort of man, with a long grey beard and soft twinkling eyes.

'Greetings!' he boomed from the stage. 'Welcome to our

Eid ball, old faces and new alike! I am pleased to have you all here to celebrate not just Eid but another successful year of harvests, alhamdulillah. We have prepared a dazzling night of entertainment and feasts, so do please enjoy yourselves!'

A round of applause erupted from the crowd. The King sat back down and a group of actors took to the stage. A tale began about a young boy and girl who fell in love with one another when they met in school.

'Layla, my Layla!' a young man cried, falling at his knees before a beautiful young woman.

'*Everybody knew of their affection for one another, but their love brought shame to their families!*' the narrator read dramatically from the side of the stage. '*The two were forbidden to see each other, and Layla was locked away . . .*'

After a few minutes, Rumaysa was wondering why they called this entertainment. The story was so depressing. She turned to say as much to Ayla, but when she looked at her friend she could see that her eyes were shining as she watched the play.

Ayla was marvelling at the unfolding tale. To be loved so passionately was something she could only dream of. Ever since her parents had passed, she had felt that there was no

117

such thing as love in her life.

After the play was over, the dancing began. The crowd spilt outwards to create a circle in the middle. The King and the Prince came into the centre and joined arms, performing a dance to the sound of drums. Soon enough, most of the crowd had joined in.

Ayla and Rumaysa stayed on the periphery, clapping along and watching the dancers with amusement. They couldn't really see the faces of the King and Prince very clearly from this far back in the crowd, but Ayla saw her stepsisters being shoved unceremoniously by their mother into the dance circle. She was hoping, no doubt, that they would catch the Prince's eye.

'Shall I go get us some more food?' Ayla asked Rumaysa, keen to get away from her stepfamily.

'That sounds great. Shall I come with you?' Rumaysa asked.

'No, no – you enjoy yourself and keep watching. I'll be back in a moment.' Ayla smiled and departed, weaving her way through the crowd towards the food stalls. She headed straight for the samosas and piled a few on to a napkin.

'Do you have enough there?'

Ayla looked round. A boy wearing an ornate mask studded with black gems was looking at her.

Ayla blushed. 'Um, yes.'

The boy laughed. 'I'm just joking.'

'Oh, right,' she said, looking away.

There was an awkward pause as he stared at her without saying anything. Then:

'Yourdressisbeautiful!' he said in one breath.

Ayla looked back round. 'Th-thank you,' she stammered.

The boy smiled at her. 'Have you been to the palace before?'

Ayla shook her head. 'No, this is my first time.'

'Are you enjoying it?'

Ayla wondered why this boy kept asking her all these questions. She really just wanted to eat her samosas, but she answered him anyway. 'Yes, I am. Have you been here before?'

'A few times,' he said casually, his golden cheeks turning red.

'Right,' Ayla said slowly.

'Sorry, I'm really terrible at this. I've never spoken to a girl like you before.' The boy was falling over his words.

Ayla found herself smiling. 'It's OK – you don't have to apologize. I find talking to new people a bit scary too.'

The boy smiled sheepishly back. He had olive-green eyes framed by dark lashes and a kind smile that Ayla found warming.

'Would you like a samosa?' Ayla offered.

'Thank you,' he said, taking one. 'I'm Harun, by the way.' He inclined his head in a bow.

'Nice to meet you,' she replied.

He looked at her curiously for a moment. 'Are you enjoying the show?' he asked, looking rather amused.

'Yes, I loved *Layla and Majnun*! It's such a beautiful story,' Ayla gushed.

He looked taken aback. 'Really? I think it's terrible. Majnun just cries about wanting to marry Layla and it being forbidden – if I were him, I would just go and get the love of my life.'

'But they hide Layla from him!' Ayla countered. 'He spends his whole life waiting for her!'

Harun grimaced. 'What kind of true love waits? You don't just wait around for someone; you have to *do* something to get them!'

'But that's the whole point – their love doesn't depend on being together or what they get from each other. They love each other regardless,' Ayla said defiantly.

Harun looked unconvinced. 'Why wish for something when you could just make it happen?'

'So what would happen in your version?' Ayla asked, offended that Harun was trying to crush her perception of Layla and Majnun.

'Get this,' Harun said excitedly. 'Majnun is forbidden to marry Layla, right? So instead of rolling over, he takes all his riches, and whatever else he needs, gets a horse, breaks Layla out and they run away to somewhere no one can find them. Job done: they all live happily ever after.'

Ayla stared at him, unimpressed. 'Where's the story in that? Did you ever think that maybe Layla could break *herself* out?'

'Would you rather they *weren't* together?' Harun said, shocked Ayla wasn't impressed by his version of events.

'No, of course I want them to end up together, but with a bit more excitement! There needs to be a battle of some sort where they fight for each other, and some difficulties on their travels before they get to live happily ever after.'

'Oh, you'd prefer to make life harder?' Harun said, laughing. 'I suppose the lucky guy who gets your hand has to slay a dragon or two before he can win your heart?'

Ayla frowned slightly and opened her mouth to reply.

'Excuse me!'

Ayla looked up and saw Rubina and Sufina, trailed discreetly by Amelia, coming towards them.

Ayla bolted.

'Wait!' Harun called after her.

'May I ask you for a dance, sir?' Rubina asked in a shrill voice.

'Oh, I don't think I'm allowed,' Harun said, looking slightly panicked. A flock of young girls was beginning to mill around.

Terrified that her stepfamily would recognize her, Ayla hurried through the crowd back to where she had been with Rumaysa. She searched through the many faces, wondering where her friend was.

Still not used to the big crowd, Rumaysa was weaving her way through the mass of dancers and onlookers, trying to find some space.

'Rumaysa!' a voice exclaimed behind her.

Rumaysa turned. Her mouth fell open as she saw Suleiman rushing towards her.

'It *is* you!' he said excitedly. 'Fancy seeing you here.'

He looked the same as when he'd left her, although his clothes were new, and he wasn't bedraggled and dirty from having dashed through a forest.

'Suleiman! How did you get here?' Rumaysa asked.

'On my carpet, of course,' Suleiman said proudly.

'Is the Princess here?' she asked.

Suleiman shook his head. 'No. I thought I'd come see what the ball was like. I haven't eaten properly in weeks – I knew there'd be some great food here.'

'I've never seen so many people before,' Rumaysa confessed quietly. 'It's amazing.'

'Of course – it must be a bit overwhelming,' Suleiman said knowingly. 'If you want to add some flavour to your samosa, try getting some yoghurt. Lovely stuff!' he said dreamily. 'And have you tried mint sauce? It's incredible.'

'Mint sauce?' Rumaysa repeated, awed. There was so much out there that she needed to discover. She wished there was a book that would just tell her everything she needed to know about the world.

'Any luck finding your parents here, then?' Suleiman asked through a mouthful of food.

Rumaysa shook her head. 'The necklace brought me to someone else.'

'Yes, bit annoying how it does that,' Suleiman replied. 'You never know where it might take you.'

Rumaysa grimaced. 'How are your injuries?'

'Oh, fine! Nothing a healer couldn't fix,' he said happily.

'There you are!' Ayla said to Rumaysa as she appeared from the crowd. 'I've been looking for you everywhere!'

'Sorry, I was just looking around,' Rumaysa said. 'This is Suleiman. He was – he's – well . . . we only met once before.'

'Pleasure to meet you!' Suleiman said heartily to Ayla.

Before Ayla could reply, Amelia was beside them. 'Excuse me, dear, I just wanted to ask where your dress is from?' she said to Ayla with a sweet smile.

Ayla stared back at her in shock. Rumaysa looked between Amelia and Ayla. Suleiman, of course, had no idea what was going on.

Ayla mouthed wordlessly at her stepmother, before she grabbed Rumaysa's hand and pulled her away, setting off at a run.

'Bye, then!' Suleiman called after Rumaysa.

Rumaysa looked over her shoulder to shout, 'Bye!' back at Suleiman. Amelia was looking confused and annoyed next to him. Ayla and Rumaysa weaved through the crowds, hurrying towards the exit.

'Miss! Where are you going?' Harun said, appearing behind them suddenly.

'I have to go!' Ayla shouted, slightly out of breath as they ran.

'When will I see you again?' he yelled after her.

People are so clingy, Rumaysa thought distractedly.

'Sorry!' was all Ayla could think to shout back.

The girls ran down the palace steps. 'Cuber!'

The carriage that had brought them to the palace sprang into action and trotted over.

'Wait, miss!' Harun called, from the top of the steps. 'At least tell me your name!'

Ayla turned back, her left foot twisting as she did so. 'Ow!' she cried as her golden shoe flew off. Rumaysa turned to get

126

it, but Ayla shouted, 'There's no time! We need to go!' She pulled Rumaysa's hand and gave Harun a helpless look before rushing into the carriage with one bare foot.

'Go – as fast as you can!' Ayla instructed the driver, fear still gripping her. If Amelia had recognized her, she was finished. She needed to get home before they did. She took a few deep breaths, and the two sat in silence all the way back to Ayla's house, each lost in their own thoughts.

VI

The two girls hurried into the manor, climbing up three flights of creaky stairs to Ayla's attic bedroom. As soon as they got into the room, they flung themselves on to the bed in happy exhaustion.

After a few moments Ayla said, 'I don't ever want to take this dress off! Tonight I got to be another person, not just an orphan girl.'

'Who was that boy that turned up at the end?' Rumaysa asked.

Ayla's face turned a delicate shade of pink. 'He – um – his name is Harun.'

Rumaysa smiled in response. 'How do you know him?'

Ayla told Rumaysa about their encounter at the food stall

128

and their conversation. Her eyes lit up as she spoke.

'Maybe you could go back to the ball . . .' Rumaysa suggested.

'No, I can't. I'm sure my stepfamily will be back soon and if I'm not here it'll mean trouble. They can't know that I was there.'

'But don't you want to see Harun again? You don't even know where he lives or how to find him.'

'That's OK,' Ayla said, touching her dress lovingly. 'Tonight was something out of a dream. I'll hold on to it forever. Besides, he looked like a wealthy boy. People like that don't mix with people like me.'

Rumaysa didn't know what to say.

Outside, the sound of a carriage approaching made Ayla sit bolt upright. She changed fast out of her ballgown, throwing on an old dress instead. Rumaysa helped her fold the dress up and tuck away the golden shoe into the bottom of a trunk.

The sound of a door slamming was followed by a shrill cry. 'Ayla! Where's our tea?'

'Just stay here – I won't be long,' Ayla whispered to Rumaysa.

Rumaysa nodded.

Ayla ran from the room and hurried down the stairs, almost skidding into the living room. She checked the time on the mantelpiece clock; it wasn't even midnight yet.

'Aren't you going to serve our tea?' Amelia demanded again. She slumped down on to a dark red armchair. 'You know I like my tea before bed.'

'I wasn't expecting you all back so soon,' Ayla said. 'I'll go and prepare it now—'

'The Prince left the ball early!' Amelia cried. 'Can you believe it? He couldn't take his eyes off that girl dressed all in gold!'

'What?' Ayla said in a small voice, shocked.

'It's true – he wouldn't take his eyes off her,' Sufina said timidly. She couldn't really meet Ayla's eyes; she was still so embarrassed by the way her mother had acted before the ball. 'She left the party and he disappeared inside the palace soon after.'

'I thought her dress was so lovely,' Rubina said, looking nervously at her mother.

'Yes, yes, she looked positively royal,' Amelia said dismissively. 'Unlike you two, who can't even catch the paper boy's eye.'

Rubina and Sufina looked hurt.

'That stupid golden girl,' Amelia grumbled, leaving the room.

Ayla was astounded.

'What did the Prince look like?' Ayla asked Rubina and Sufina casually, once Amelia was out of earshot.

'Oh, he's so handsome!' Rubina squealed in hushed tones. 'He has these beautiful dark locks and lovely green eyes—'

'He was wearing these fancy navy robes and a matching mask!' Sufina proclaimed. 'He's so dashing, I might just *die* from his beauty!'

Ayla's mind ran round in circles. Harun. *Harun was the Prince?* She had spent all that time talking to the *Prince*?

She couldn't believe it.

'Hurry up, girl!' Amelia's voice barked at her.

Once Ayla had made the hot drinks, she walked back up to her room in a daze, wanting to tell Rumaysa what she had just learned about Harun. But when Ayla entered the attic she saw the other girl was fast asleep on top of the covers. Ayla smiled and pulled a blanket over her. They could talk about it in the morning.

'Ayla?' There was a knock on her door. 'Ayla, are you OK?' It was Sufina's voice.

Ayla went to the door and cracked it open a tiny bit, making sure that Rumaysa was shielded from view. 'What are you doing here?' she asked.

Sufina was flanked by Rubina. 'I'm sorry Mother ruined your dress, you know, before the ball.'

'Yeah, we're sorry,' Rubina said quietly.

Ayla stared in surprise. 'Why are you apologizing?'

'Because,' Sufina said uncomfortably, averting her grey eyes, 'some things are just not right. But I think Mother takes all her anger out on you, and it's not fair.'

Rubina nodded in agreement.

'Thanks, I suppose. That's very kind of you.' Ayla was touched. Her stepsisters had never been so open with her before, especially not about their mother.

'We brought you some sweets from the ball because you didn't get to go,' Sufina said, pulling a small paper bag from her cloak and handing it to Ayla. She and Rubina scurried off back downstairs.

Ayla made sure to lock her door. She sat down on the edge of her bed and poked at the sweets. Today had been such a bizarre day. Her dress had been ruined by Amelia, then she had met Rumaysa, got a brand-new dress, spoken to the

Prince of Qamaroon and apparently caught his eye! And now Sufina and Rubina were giving her sweets!

She couldn't believe the day had been real. Ayla wished she could tell her mother all about it. She made a little bed for herself on an old chaise and settled in, hugging a picture of her parents to her chest as her eyes slowly closed.

The next morning, Ayla was unceremoniously awakened by her stepmother yelling up the stairs for her breakfast. She made her way downstairs to prepare the tea and pastries for her stepfamily, leaving their portion in the kitchen and sneaking the rest upstairs to share with Rumaysa.

'There's something I need to tell you,' Ayla said excitedly as she sat back down on her bed, offering Rumaysa a muffin.

Rumaysa took one. '*Whab-is-it?*' she asked through a crumbly mouthful of sweet dough and blueberries. It was delicious.

Ayla quickly relayed all the information she'd discovered from her stepfamily, trying not to squeal.

'So, the boy you spoke to is the Prince?' Rumaysa said, shocked.

Ayla nodded.

'You should go back to the palace!' Rumaysa said eagerly.

Ayla shrugged, a sad smile appearing on her face. 'There's no point. I mean, he's the Prince! I'm just . . . well, me.'

'Ayla, get down here!' Amelia yelled from downstairs.

Rumaysa and Ayla shared a look.

Ayla sighed. 'Ugh.'

'Ayla! Immediately! Now!'

Ayla grudgingly went down.

'Where's my dress? You haven't ironed it yet! I have a very important lunch to go to!'

'You didn't tell me to iron your dress,' Ayla said blankly.

'Well, go and find one!' she snapped.

Ayla had half a mind to remind Amelia how she had destroyed her own dress, but thought perhaps she would just let the iron burn through the Amelia's instead.

Suddenly the sound of a bell ringing came from outside, and all four of their heads whipped towards the window.

'Attention, all residents!' a voice boomed.

Rubina leaped towards the window. 'That's the royal guard!'

Amelia jumped out of her seat and rushed to

join Rubina. 'What are they doing? Open the window!' she snapped.

Rubina quickly threw the window wide open.

'His Royal Highness, Prince Harun, has commanded us to find the girl in the golden dress from last night's ball. She left behind a shoe. Should she come forward, she must try on this slipper to prove herself!'

'My shoe!' Ayla whispered, her hand flying to her mouth in surprise.

Amelia's head swivelled towards her. 'What did you say?'

Ayla froze. 'Um, I said *hachoo*! I sneezed,' she said quickly.

'I want to go and see!' Rubina said, hurrying out of the room.

'I'm coming too!' Sufina added excitedly, rushing to the front door with her.

Ayla took her cue to head back to her room. But just as she reached the parlour door, Amelia clasped her hand around Ayla's wrist and yanked her back.

'What did you say?' she growled at Ayla.

'I told you – I sneezed,' Ayla replied, trying to shake her grip.

'Liar,' Amelia hissed. 'You said, "My shoe." I heard you!'

'No, I didn't – I swear,' Ayla said desperately.

Amelia's nostrils flared. 'Deceitful child! After I forbade you to go, you disobeyed me!'

'No, I didn't! Please!' Ayla shouted.

Amelia pulled Ayla up the stairs and threw her into her room.

'You will not try on that shoe – do you hear me?' Amelia shouted. 'You will stay in here until I decide to let you out!'

Ayla stared back at Amelia in horror. 'Please, no—'

Amelia slammed the door shut. There was a loud rattling as she locked the door with a key.

'No! Please, Amelia! I didn't do anything, please!' Ayla begged, throwing herself at the door. 'Amelia! Amelia, please!'

'What's going on?' Rumaysa asked, poking her head up from under the bed where she'd been hiding.

'She knows it was me,' Ayla said, tears springing to her eyes. 'She knows I went to the ball!'

Rumaysa looked back at her with dread. 'We need to get out of here and get to the Prince,' she said decisively.

'But how will we get out?' Ayla sniffed, wiping her tears. She wanted her parents so much in that moment.

Rumaysa looked at the window. Then at Ayla's bedsheets.

VII

'Are you sure this will work?' Ayla whispered fearfully as Rumaysa knotted together all the old blankets and sheets they'd found in Ayla's room.

Rumaysa tugged on the makeshift rope. It seemed strong. 'Quick, put your cloak on while I tie this to the end of your bed.'

Rumaysa felt a wave of déjà vu as she wrapped one end of the rope around Ayla's bedframe a few times before securing it with another knot. She couldn't believe she was doing this again.

Ayla had her cloak on and looked ready, if a little frightened. Rumaysa grabbed hers too and pushed the window open as wide as she could. She hauled herself over the ledge and began to climb down. It was definitely less scary than climbing out of her tower.

She landed on the ground with a hard thud. 'Come on!' she whispered up to Ayla.

Ayla wasn't quite as good as Rumaysa at the whole 'climbing down the side of a building' thing. Just before she reached the ground, her grip on the sheets slipped and, with a loud gasp, she fell the last few feet. Rumaysa put out her arms to catch her, and the two girls stumbled slightly but managed to keep their feet.

They turned and saw a crowd had gathered on the street.

'We will try it on!' Amelia was yelling, so focused on the King's carriages that she hadn't noticed two girls scaling down the side of her house.

A crowd milled around the royal carriage, and a frenzy erupted as Prince Harun emerged. Ayla froze, transfixed.

'Form a line – form a line!' a guard ordered, waving a stick menacingly.

A line quickly formed, full of shoving, as every girl on the road waited to try on the shoe. Amelia pushed Rubina and Sufina forward first, elbowing a few people back as she did so.

Rubina tried on the shoe reluctantly with her mother breathing down her neck. She barely got three toes in before the shoe began to cut at her feet.

'Try harder!' her mother hissed.

Rubina winced as she tried to squeeze her foot in, but her fourth toe wouldn't fit. She yanked her foot out and fell back on to the grass, gasping with relief.

'Sufina, put it on!' Amelia insisted, practically shoving her other daughter's foot into the shoe. Amelia twisted Sufina's foot this way and that, but it wouldn't work.

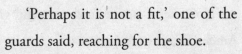

'Perhaps it is not a fit,' one of the guards said, reaching for the shoe.

'No – just give us a moment!' Amelia said tersely, continuing to ram her daughter's foot into the unyielding shoe.

'Mother, I can't feel my foot!' Sufina moaned as it began to turn red. 'Stop!' She jerked away.

Sufina's foot hit her mother square in the mouth and sent them both toppling backwards.

Barely a second passed before they were buried in the crowd as their neighbours rushed forward. Everyone squeezed and pushed and cried, but nobody's foot could fit the perfectly sculpted shoe. Ayla supposed that was part of Rumaysa's magic.

'You there,' the guard, a tall woman, said, looking over at Ayla and Rumaysa as they approached. 'Will you try on the shoe?'

Out of the corner of her eye, Ayla saw Amelia's head swing round. Her eyes widened in disbelief as she recognized her stepdaughter. Before Ayla could reply, Amelia lunged forward.

'No! She is just a lowly servant girl! Get back inside!' Amelia hissed to Ayla.

'I asked her, not you,' the guard said.

Hearing the commotion, Harun came forward, looking between Amelia and Ayla. She looked back intently, her eyes filled with hope.

'Do we know each other?' Harun asked, looking at Ayla suspiciously.

Ayla felt that small spark of hope flicker and fade. Of course, he didn't recognize her.

'Ayla, tell him who you are,' Rumaysa whispered, nudging her with her elbow.

'I-I'm the one who wore gold to your ball – the one you spoke to.'

Harun's eyebrows knitted together in a frown. He looked her up and down, taking in her worn clothes and unbrushed hair, his eyes distasteful.

'She's lying! *I'm* the girl you spoke to!' Tahmina, the girl next door said, running towards them and falling at Harun's feet. 'Your Majesty!'

'No – it's my daughter!' Amelia protested, trying to shoo the girl away with one hand and pull Sufina in with the other.

Harun looked haughtily at them all. 'What is going on here?'

'Perhaps the young lady ought to try on the shoe?' the guard said.

'Your Highness, these girls are liars! They are thieves! They have been terrorizing our neighbourhood, posing as beggars and stealing everything in sight!' Amelia proclaimed.

'That's not true!' Rumaysa exclaimed in outrage. 'Ayla, say something!'

But Ayla couldn't speak. For the look in Harun's eyes – the distaste, the . . . disappointment – had made her shrink inside herself.

'I think you ought to try it on,' the guard said, putting the shoe before Ayla. She gave an encouraging smile as Ayla slowly lifted her foot.

The entire crowd gasped as her foot slipped in easily.

Harun looked at Ayla in sudden shock. 'Is it really you? But how can it be?'

'No! This is witchcraft!' Amelia cried.

'If you speak one more time, I'll arrest you for obstructing the Prince!' the guard barked at Amelia.

Amelia fell silent, abashed.

Ayla looked at Harun.

'Who are you?' he asked.

'My name is Ayla,' she replied. Ayla wasn't sure what this strange pain was in her chest, but it felt like betrayal. He didn't recognize her. Was she that much of a nobody just because her clothes looked grey and worn?

Next to her, Rumaysa was fuming. How dare he look at Ayla like she was nothing? She shouldn't have to make Ayla another dress for him to realize that she was worth talking to!

'What were you doing at that house?' Prince Harun asked, looking at the rope behind Ayla and Rumaysa.

'It's my house. Well, my father's house,' she said. 'My father died a year ago. My stepmother and stepsisters live there too.' She gestured towards her stepfamily on her left.

'Is this true?' Harun demanded of Amelia.

Amelia nodded. 'Y-yes, Your Majesty.'

'So why did you say she was a thief?'

Amelia blanched.

'She doesn't want you to know I'm the girl in the golden dress. She tried to lock me in my room,' Ayla said in a stronger voice.

The crowd gasped again, shocked whispers flying through them.

'That's not true!' Amelia said.

'It is, Mother,' said Sufina in a quiet voice. Rubina was nodding beside her.

'You would lie to your own prince?' Harun said, drawing himself up to his full height. Rumaysa looked at him disgruntledly. *What a show-off!*

'Nazia, arrest this woman,' Harun ordered. 'A night or two in prison will sort her out, and when she's released, see to it that she never enters this household again!'

The guard stepped forward and produced handcuffs. The crowd looked on in shock as Amelia was taken away, protesting loudly.

'So, it *is* you,' Harun said, looking back at Ayla. 'But you're not a princess.'

'I never said I was,' Ayla said in a stilted voice.

'Right. Yes. I suppose you didn't,' he said matter-of-factly.

Ayla felt something cold taking over her insides.

The Prince smiled. 'Well, I'm pleased to know who you are – who you *really* are.'

Ayla wasn't sure she felt the same.

'I don't think my father will be best pleased that you aren't a princess, but I'm sure I can talk him round,' Harun said with a new, excited energy. 'You are very beautiful, and perhaps with your stepmother out of the picture you can resume a more noble life and outlook.'

Rumaysa and Ayla shared a confused glance, before Ayla said, 'Sorry, what?'

'Ayla, mystery girl from the ball, owner of the lost shoe,' Harun proclaimed, getting down on one knee. 'Will you marry me?'

The crowd gasped (again).

'What?' Ayla spluttered once more.

'I have not stopped thinking about you since the ball – I can't even sleep,' Harun professed.

Ayla looked at him incredulously. 'Wasn't the ball just yesterday?'

'Yes, but a day is like a thousand years without my beloved,' he said with anguish.

'You just looked at me like I was dirt because my clothes are worn!' Ayla said.

Harun faltered. 'I-I was just shocked!'

'No, you were just honest,' Ayla said firmly. 'A thousand apologies for causing you to lose sleep, Your Highness. I hope you will sleep better tonight now you know what a simple girl I am and that you needn't worry your father. Good day.' And with that, she turned her back on the prince and marched away.

'I can get you new clothes?' Harun called after her.

'I like mine how they are!' Ayla retorted over her shoulder.

Harun was left looking rather lost and stupid, still on one knee, as Ayla stalked back inside her house. Rumaysa followed, as did Rubina and Sufina, more tentatively.

Behind them, they could hear the guards ushering the crowd away. 'Come on, folks – show's over. Back to your homes.'

'So, you're not going to marry the Prince?' Rubina asked tentatively.

'No! He's so rude!' Ayla fumed. 'And we're far too young to get married! What was he thinking?'

'He doesn't actually look that handsome up close and in the light,' Rubina said very disappointedly.

'He doesn't seem like a nice person up close, either,' Rumaysa said with a grimace.

'Agreed,' Sufina replied.

All four girls shared a smile.

'Ayla,' Rubina said slowly, 'will you kick us out now?'

Ayla looked at the twins in confusion. 'Do you want to live here?'

They both shrugged, looking a bit afraid.

146

'Don't you want to live with your mother?' Ayla asked.

Sufina and Rubina shared a look. 'I think she needs to be on her own for a while,' Sufina said. 'She hasn't been her usual self for a long, long time.'

Rubina nodded. 'We feel really bad for how she treated you. We know we weren't any better, either.'

'You can stay,' Ayla said slowly. 'But I'm never lifting a finger for either of you again.'

'Oh, thank you, thank you!' they both said, grabbing Ayla for a hug.

'I'll make you breakfast for a year!' Rubina said.

'And I'll make you lunch!' Sufina promised.

Ayla laughed, her eyes filling with tears.

Rumaysa watched the three of them fondly, feeling a swell of relief for Ayla. Against her chest, the necklace began to throb. She pulled it out to see that it was pulsing with its strange purple light again.

'I think I have to go,' Rumaysa said, as a familiar magnetic pull began to surround her.

'Oh, please stay!' Ayla said. 'You can live here too! Please?' She enveloped Rumaysa in a hug. 'You're the best person I've ever met!'

Rumaysa felt tears sting her eyes as she hugged Ayla back. 'I would love to. But I have to find my parents.'

They pulled apart sadly and Ayla nodded. 'I'll be praying for you,' she said.

Rumaysa wiped away a few stray tears and smiled. 'Thank you so much. I've never had a real human friend before. You've been so kind.'

'Please come back one day – promise?' Ayla said.

Before Rumaysa could reply, she felt herself being sucked into a spinning whirlpool as everything around her went dark.

Ayla and her stepsisters stared in shock as Rumaysa disappeared in a puff of purple smoke.

'Whoa,' Sufina said. 'Who was that?'

'Rumaysa,' Ayla said with a smile. 'She's magic.'

The mood in the house was bittersweet over the next few days as they all adjusted to life without Amelia. Ayla had a newfound joy of being in her home, something she hadn't felt for years. Though it wasn't the same as being with her parents, the absence of Amelia seemed to free the house of its bad energy, and Ayla was able to restore all the old furniture with the help of her stepsisters.

It wasn't entirely easy for the three of them to adapt to this new life together, but it felt a lot nicer than the life they were living before. Rubina discovered she was an amazing cook, and Sufina found herself to be a very talented mathematician as she began to do her own schoolwork. And Ayla could now do anything she wanted or dared to dream of.

Sleeping Sara

I

Once upon a time, there lived a king and a queen who ruled over the land of Farisia. They were not the best of rulers. Harsh winters and dry summers had led King Emad and Queen Shiva to tax their people highly, without relief, and the people of Farisia could barely make ends meet. There were some who tried to hide crops or save their pennies from the tax collectors, but even that was not enough.

The King was a short man with dark hair and darker eyes. The Queen was tall with fiery-red hair and hazel eyes. Everyone thought she was a beautiful woman, but, as time passed, her face grew sadder and sadder. For, after years of marriage, the rulers still had no children.

As the kingdom continued to fail and still there was no

heir, dissent among the people grew. The King was afraid of losing his throne. With no child to continue his reign, it seemed as though the people had in mind their own ideas for a ruler.

But as fate would have it, one night, when the stars were especially bright, the Queen discovered she was with child. She and the King couldn't believe it; after years of trying, it seemed a miracle had happened.

Queen Shiva began making preparations immediately. She instructed her servants to build the finest nursery in the land, with the most lavish furnishings and all the toys imaginable. The King was beside himself with joy, delighted that his reign was secured.

On one hot summer's day, the Queen gave birth to a baby girl. She held the child in her arms and was overcome by a wave of love. 'Hello, little one,' she whispered.

'She has my nose,' the King said softly, his eyes welling up. 'My heir.'

Shiva looked at her husband and smiled. 'We shall call her Sara.'

King Emad called for an announcement to be made across the entire kingdom. Swathes of people went to the palace with gifts, hoping to catch a glimpse of the royal family from their balcony, but the palace gates were shut. Disgruntled, the people left, hoping they would get to see the child another time.

But it was not to be, for the King and Queen had finally gotten their child, and they would do anything to protect her. Ever mindful of the dissenters and unrest outside, they decided to keep their precious daughter safely inside the palace grounds.

Days turned into weeks and soon enough into months. The people of Farisia waited and waited, but there was no sight of the new child.

As the years passed and the King grew older, whispers grew that his daughter would soon be ruling the kingdom. People said that the girl was kept locked away because she was unfit to rule. That she had been cursed as a baby. That she wasn't even the true heir.

The people of Farisia did not want such a child on their throne. Protests grew worse across the land. The King sent his soldiers to dispel each uprising, but more would rise in new locations. King Emad, instead of finding compassion for his people's troubles, only found anger at their disrespect for his laws. He put harsh punishments in place for even the quietest of dissenters.

There was one man who decided to use the unrest in Farisia to his advantage. A thin, reedy man with long, dark hair and a beard that reached down to his knees, Azra wanted nothing more than to sit on the throne. He felt that there were too many rules in place, and he did not enjoy paying his taxes (though he *was* a man of the people). Driven to desperation by the situation, the revolters looked to him to lead. But they were fearful of him too.

For Azra practised dark magic and used it to control the dragons that lived in the northern mountains of Farisia. These great winged beasts were unpredictable, and people kept away from them. But Azra tamed them for his own use, and the dragons knew to fear his evil magic and cruelty.

Most feared of all was a beast called Griselda, who was monstrously huge and had scaly black skin that gleamed purple in the light. Azra bound her to him through his dark power, and he used her to strike fear into the hearts of his followers so that no one would dare disobey him.

News of the so-called Dragon Man and his supporters reached the palace. The King and Queen ordered their generals to put a stop to Azra, but he was a slippery man who knew how to evade capture. The key to dissenting was to not be obvious, obviously.

The people of Farisia came to see their rulers as cruel and cold-hearted. Several plots failed to ambush the King on the few times he left the palace, but the King's guards were the best of the best. They foiled the revolters at every turn, but, even so, the King left the palace less and less. Unwilling to risk anything happening to Sara, the King and Queen saw no choice but to start sheltering themselves. Eventually it had been years since anyone in the land of Farisia had seen any member of the royal family.

And Azra bade his time, patiently waiting for the perfect opportunity to strike.

II

As unrest grew outside its walls, inside the palace Princess Sara was turning into an intelligent and headstrong girl. She had her mother's eyes and her father's warm, brown skin and dark, wavy hair. Sara had a beautiful big body that was always dressed in the finest robes; she always had the best toys to play with and received an education from the most respected tutors in the land. The young princess could want for no material thing.

Unable to go outside, Sara spent her days exploring the palace. She was an adventurous girl, who passed all hours of the day and night roaming the vast corridors and huge, empty rooms. She had a particular fascination with the dungeons and loved how the dark and damp hallways were lit by wax candles that cast long, scary shadows as she walked. She was convinced there was a ghost down there, or secret passages waiting to be discovered.

The palace staff, from the cooks to the guards, took pity on the girl. They were all very fond of their curious, endearing princess and enjoyed playing games with her when they could. But duty often called, and Sara would once again be left on her own.

As Sara grew, so did her longing to experience life outside the palace. She often asked her parents why she wasn't allowed beyond the palace walls, but they would just tell her that the world was dangerous and that she had everything she could ever want inside the palace.

Sara couldn't make her parents understand that she didn't want *things*. She had thoroughly explored the entire palace; she knew the various courtyards inside and out, the secret rooms, the kitchens where she could get extra treats. What she wanted, more than anything, was an adventure.

The one time of year that the Princess really looked forward to was her birthday. For the King and Queen knew that their beloved daughter was lonely, so they did everything they could

to make the occasion extra special. They had spent weeks and weeks preparing for Sara's upcoming birthday, and everything was set for a magnificent party – of course, the guest list was small, but no cost was spared.

The evening before the celebrations, Sara was caught trying to peek at her cake and was shooed out of the kitchen by the head cook. She ran along the marble floors to the great hall where the servants were setting up decorations, but a guard named Amir caught her snooping and sent her on her way.

'Oh, but please – can I just see?' she wheedled, trying to see past Amir as he stood in front of the doors.

'Your Majesty, it's meant to be a surprise!' He laughed.

'Oh, come on!' She gave a winning smile. 'Please can I just look a little bit?'

'Sara, what are you doing?' her father called from behind her.

Sara turned round guiltily. 'Nothing, Baba. I was just . . . walking.'

He looked down at her with raised brows. 'Really? You weren't trying to sneak into the hall to see the decorations?'

161

'Decorations? What for, Baba?' Sara said innocently.

The King smiled knowingly at her. 'Come along with me, young lady.'

Sara sighed and followed her father away from the great hall and to the study where her mother also sat, working. No doubt King Emad was about to give her another one of his speeches about behaving more responsibly.

'You know, Sara,' the King began, 'one day soon you will rule this kingdom.' He sat down at his desk. 'We will have to increase your education and training so you'll be ready when that time comes.'

Sara flung herself into a chair. 'It's a lot for one person to rule a kingdom, isn't it, Father? I think *you* should just keep doing it.' Sara had no interest in ruling. In her daydreams she liked to imagine a different life for herself. Currently, she was considering being a lion tamer.

'I will not live forever, my child,' her father replied with a small smile.

'You will make an excellent queen, dear,' Queen Shiva said over her papers, smiling fondly at her daughter. 'The people of Farisia will be lucky to have you rule them.'

'But I don't even know who the people of Farisia are.' Sara

sighed and folded her arms. 'Will I get to go outside the palace when I am queen?'

'Well, you'll get to know them somehow,' the King said shortly. 'Have you got any more presents that you want? Baba will make anything happen for you.'

Sara sensed her father's discomfort. Her parents always got cagey when she mentioned anything to do with the outside. She had been sure they were both about to have a heart attack when she'd asked to go to the zoo as a birthday treat last year. Instead, she'd been gifted a number of animals to make her own sanctuary in one of the palace gardens. But Sara had felt bad for how small a space the animals had, and she'd quietly freed them. It had taken a number of days for the palace guards to round them all up from the city. Her parents had been furious.

'No, I don't want anything else, thank you,' Sara replied, glancing over at one of the globes atop the fireplace. She got up and walked over to it, reaching out a hand to gently spin it, looking at all the different countries across the world as it rotated. She wished she could get out and see some of them.

After dinner, Sara bid her parents goodnight and retired to her bedroom, while the King and Queen went to finalize everything for the next day's celebrations. Everyone in the palace had been enlisted to help, abandoning their usual posts.

Sara sighed as she changed out of her blue gown and into a more comfortable nightdress. She wasn't sure why she had to wear such grand dresses at home, given that the only people she saw were the servants, but apparently it was what royals did. Perhaps she should have asked for simpler clothes for her birthday.

Sara wondered what her life would have been like if she'd never been a princess. Perhaps she could have grown up with siblings or friends, played outside and explored the land of Farisia. It wasn't that she was unhappy with her life here – she was grateful for everything she had – but her parents smothered her.

She climbed into bed and began to drift off to sleep, lost in thought . . .

What felt like moments later, Sara was startled awake by a sudden noise outside her window. She stayed still for a moment, listening out, but all was quiet.

She rolled over in her large bed and tried to get back to sleep.

Crash!

Sara bolted upright. One of her windows had been smashed, letting in a swell of cold night air. Fragments of glass littered her floor. A thick, large scaly tail slithered back from the window as she watched, open mouthed.

She yelled and jumped back, staring through the broken glass in horror – hanging in the air, right outside her window, was a huge black dragon. Its wings flapped slowly and menacingly up and down as its big red snakelike eyes appeared to block out the night sky. They bored into Sara and she froze, unable to shout out or move.

The Princess stared transfixed as the red of Griselda the dragon's irises took over her vision. The dark magic filled her, seeping into her body and taking hold of her mind. Her limbs began to weaken. Her eyes strained, blurring, and eventually everything turned black.

Sara fell into a deep, deep slumber.

Far below, the guards on the ground saw the beast outside the Princess's window and alarm bells rang throughout the palace. Griselda ignored the arrows that bounced harmlessly off her scales and reached in through the window with a huge claw. Her talons enclosed the bewitched Princess. She gripped the girl tightly and launched immediately into the sky, flapping her great bat-like wings as chaos ensued in the palace.

The King and Queen heard the noise and ran without thought towards their daughter's chambers. Panic filled them as they reached her door, only to find her bedroom floor covered in shards of glass and their precious child gone.

Alarm bells were rung across the entire land as the soldiers raided every house, every shop, every inn looking for Sara. News of the missing princess spread like wildfire through the land, much to everyone's shock and horror. Not even the most loyal dissenters had known of Azra's heinous plans to steal the Princess.

Azra himself patiently watched the fire he had set erupt. And when he deemed the time was right, he arrived at the palace on the back of a midnight-blue dragon.

His demands were simple, really. The King and Queen were to give up their throne and surrender to him, and Sara would be returned. King Emad and Queen Shiva fearfully agreed, but as soon as their guards stood down, Azra's henchmen threw every last one of them into the dungeon. Azra had lied to them, and he intended that the King and Queen would spend the rest of their days locked beneath the palace floors.

As the new King of Farisia was announced, the people rejoiced, glad to be free of their terrible rulers.

All seemed hopeful at first. But, very soon, the people of Farisia came to realize the promises Azra had made to them were empty. As the months passed, bad harvests continued to plague the land, and Azra increased their taxes even more than King Emad had done. More and more people were falling into poverty, but no one dared to stand up to Azra with his fearsome dragons constantly prowling the skies.

King Emad and Queen Shiva wasted away in their dungeon, hoping and praying for some news of their daughter, not knowing that far, far away, a sleeping Sara lay in darkness.

III

Rumaysa found herself spiralling out of a purple hole and landing with a hard thud on rocky ground. She scrambled to her feet and dusted herself down.

'Why don't you give me softer landing?' she grumbled.

The necklace ignored her.

Rumaysa looked around properly. She was standing at the base of a very large rock formation, it seemed. In the distance she could see more of these strange enormous mounds.

Mountains! she suddenly realized. That's what they were called.

'Wow,' she breathed. It was rather beautiful, standing in a valley surrounded by mountains, with the clear blue sky above her. She was enjoying drinking in all the scenery when the necklace gave a tug in her hand. Rumaysa reluctantly looked down. It was leading her towards a trail that began at the very bottom of the mountain.

She glared at the necklace again. 'You'd better find me my parents, or I'm putting you in the bin.' The necklace crackled, stinging her faintly.

'Ow!' Rumaysa cursed, shaking the pain from her hand. The necklace flickered its purple light, as if laughing.

'*Now* you communicate,' Rumaysa grumbled. 'If you can understand me, why aren't you doing what I ask?'

The necklace was still.

Rumaysa glowered at it and then started walking.

She walked for what felt like hours. As she climbed higher up the mountain, she could see more and more of the scenery around her. There were endless emerald trees separated by great lakes that looked like little turquoise pools from where she was.

The glow of the necklace began to fade as Rumaysa reached the top. She wiped her sweaty face on the back of her sleeve; she had never walked so much in her life. Her legs felt achy and there was a stitch in her side. She wished she had brought some water with her.

Rumaysa half collapsed on to the ground and lay on her back, panting. As she looked around the sky, the peak of an enormous dark turret caught her eye. She blinked a few times . . . Was she hallucinating?

The turret stayed in place. Rumaysa scrambled back to her sore feet and walked further up the trail, to find that the turret sat atop a small tower that protruded out of the grey mountain rock.

'Really?' Rumaysa said, exasperated. 'Am I just meant to be climbing buildings for the rest of my life now?'

The necklace gave a tug as if to say yes.

The tower was small, definitely climbable, and thankfully nowhere near as high as the one Rumaysa had lived in. She grumbled to herself as she neared it, knowing deep down in her heart that her parents probably weren't here.

When she arrived at the foot of the tower, Rumaysa looked for a door of some sort, but there was nothing except a lone window right at the top. 'Do all evil people just like towers and one window?' she said out loud, feeling quite frustrated by now. 'What's the point of being evil if you're not going to be creative about it?'

The tower was made of large mismatched stones, which looked a bit unstable. 'Here goes nothing,' Rumaysa muttered, putting the necklace on once more.

She began to climb, grabbing on to the stones that stuck out and trying to hold her footing on any gaps in the wall. She wished that Zabina were with her. Somehow things seemed easier to bear with a friend to share the load.

As Rumaysa neared the top, she noticed a deep sort of rumbling sound. She looked around in confusion, but couldn't see where it was coming from. Cautiously, she kept climbing, but froze just as she reached the window. The dark turret of the tower she'd seen before was scaly, with purple streaks. It looked like it was moving up and down, as though it were breathing.

Rumaysa squinted. Was the turret . . . *snoring*?

A soft trail of fire came spiralling out of the other side of the tower. Rumaysa yelped and almost lost her footing, realizing with horror that the turret was actually a massive creature. It was dark and scaly, with large wings folded by its side, huge talons on its legs and a thick tail that was curled possessively round the top of the tower.

Rumaysa gaped. She ran through various stories in her mind as she tried to place it.

'Dragon,' she whispered after a moment.

Rumaysa had never seen such a thing in her life. Fear and panic swelled in her chest and, as if sensing her unease, the necklace gave a comforting tug.

Steeling herself, Rumaysa very carefully pulled herself up on to the window ledge, making sure to avoid the spiky tail. She managed to haul herself over and landed, as quietly as she could, in a very small, dark room. Rumaysa's eyes immediately fell upon a narrow wooden bed with a person lying on it.

'Hello?' Rumaysa called in a hushed voice. 'Excuse me?'

The figure didn't stir.

Rumaysa peered around the room. It smelt like musty rock and, apart from the bed, it was entirely bare. As she edged tentatively closer, she could see it was a young girl lying on the grubby mattress. She was wearing the prettiest nightdress Rumaysa had ever seen, a sleeved silk gown in a rich blue colour. Her reddish-brown hair was tied in two loose plaits. She looked troubled as she slept, her warm brown face set in a worried grimace as a soft snoring came from her mouth.

'Hello?' Rumaysa tried in a louder whisper. 'Hello!'

She poked the girl.

The girl carried on sleeping.

'Excuse me!' Rumaysa flapped her hand in front of the sleeping girl's face. 'You really ought to wake up! There's a dragon outside!'

The girl grunted a louder snore in response.

Rumaysa grimaced. She could see some drool coming out of the girl's mouth.

She drew back, confused as to what to do. From the state of the empty room, she was clearly being kept prisoner. Rumaysa was starting to think that the girl was in some sort of magical sleep. But how to wake her up?

She looked down at her hands. If magic were keeping her asleep, maybe magic could wake her up? *Well, there's no harm in trying*, she reasoned. It wasn't like the girl was going anywhere.

Rumaysa closed her eyes and tried to connect with the light that lived inside her. She could feel its small glow in her centre and allowed it to spread through her body, filling her completely.

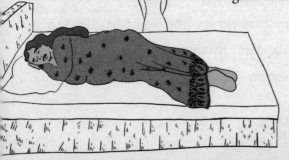

Rumaysa's hands began to shake. She turned back towards the sleeping girl and held her palms out to her.

A soft golden light emanated from her hands and swept over the girl. Rumaysa grounded her feet as the magic rushed out of her, her body shaking with the weight of it all.

The sleeping girl gave a startled grunt . . . and turned in her sleep.

Rumaysa pulled her magic back. She toppled over, falling against the wall, panting hard.

'Er, hello?' Rumaysa said.

'Not now, Mother,' the girl mumbled back. 'Five more minutes . . .'

'You really need to wake up,' Rumaysa called urgently. *What was* wrong *with this girl?*

'Shush,' the girl groaned, her voice thick with sleep. Then she started snoring very loudly again.

Rumaysa sat on the floor, perplexed.

'Rumaysa!' a voice whispered.

Rumaysa whirled around. She couldn't believe her eyes. There, at the window, was Suleiman. Floating on his carpet.

'What are you doing here?' Rumaysa asked in a hushed voice, scrambling to her feet.

'I found the Princess!' he said excitedly. He clambered into the room just as the girl on the bed gave another huge yawn, rubbing her eyes. 'Oh. You found her before me. How did you do that? Why aren't you looking for your parents?' Suleiman looked a bit annoyed.

'Well, your necklace keeps bringing me to everybody but them!' Rumaysa whispered back, also annoyed.

Suleiman groaned. 'My parents are going to be *so* disappointed in me . . . Though nothing new there.'

'Stop talking . . . Five . . . minutes,' the girl moaned from the bed.

'What's wrong with her?' Suleiman asked, looking at the Princess in alarm.

'She was under a sleeping spell, I think,' Rumaysa said. 'I think I woke her up, but . . . maybe she likes to sleep a lot.'

'Well, we should get out of here quick. That dragon outside might wake up!' Suleiman said.

The girl sighed and groggily pushed herself up from her bed. She could barely open her eyes. 'What's going on?' she asked through another great yawn.

Rumaysa and Suleiman shared a confused look.

Suleiman cleared his throat as if to announce himself.

'Your Highness, I'm here to take you home.'

The girl blinked a few times. 'Who are you?'

'I'm Suleiman, Your Highness,' Suleiman said. 'That's Rumaysa. I thought I saw you climbing up,' he added, looking at Rumaysa.

The girl looked back at them blearily in response.

'Are you Princess Sara?' Suleiman prompted as the girl's eyes threatened to close again.

'Y-yes,' she said through a great yawn.

'If you saw me, why didn't you offer me a ride on your carpet?' Rumaysa demanded from Suleiman, her voice increasing in volume. 'You could have saved me climbing this tower!'

'I wasn't sure it was really you!' he said defensively.

'You *always* show up at the wrong time,' Rumaysa said loudly, annoyed beyond belief.

'*Shh!*' Suleiman hissed, his eyes widening in urgency.

A deep rumbling sound echoed all around them.

'What's . . . that?' Sara asked sleepily, slowly sinking back into the bed.

'We should get out of here,' Rumaysa urged as another thunderous yawn erupted in the sky. 'I think the dragon is waking up.'

Suleiman nodded. 'Princess Sara, we need to leave.'

But Sara was snoring again, her mouth hanging open.

'We haven't got time – help me get her on your carpet,' Rumaysa said, rushing over to the Princess.

As they frantically hoisted a very disorientated Sara on to the magic carpet, the roof of the tower started to shake. A thick tail swooped past the window, causing Rumaysa and Suleiman to freeze in terror.

A pair of large red eyes with thin black pupils appeared in the window.

'Why is the sky red?' Sara asked confusedly.

The dragon's eyes widened with anger as it saw the three children. It let out a roar of rage that showed off every one of its razor-sharp teeth.

'Uh oh,' Rumaysa whispered.

'Go, carpet!' Suleiman yelled. Rumaysa held on to Sara with one hand and the carpet with the other as it lurched forward, twisting sideways to make it out of the small window. Behind them the dragon took in a huge, ominous breath. It spat out a barrel of flames that pummelled into the window, charring the bricks to dust.

Rumaysa and Suleiman screamed, the trail of fire narrowly missing them. A pungent smell of burning filled the air, and the carpet dashed away as they clung on for dear life, but the dragon was just as quick.

'Go, go, *go!*' Suleiman shouted frantically.

The carpet made a deep dive as another wave of flames came rushing towards them.

'It's ruining my carpet!' Suleiman exclaimed as some of the tassels on the carpet were caught by a lick of flame. Suleiman swatted at them manically, trying to put them out.

'At least it's not us!' Rumaysa shouted back, desperately trying to cling on to both the sleeping girl and the carpet.

The dragon soared towards them, screeching an awful, angry cry that made their eardrums shake.

Rumaysa looked around desperately as they tunnelled through the wind; they were hundreds of feet above the ground and the dragon was right behind them. Its grand wings stretched across the sky, blocking the sun.

In desperation, Rumaysa reached inside herself and found a song of stolen moments and crackling fires. The dragon veered slightly as it sensed Rumaysa's magic reaching out. The lull of her song was soft and inviting, but Rumaysa's magic wasn't strong enough; Griselda was too submerged in Azra's darkness. The dragon's red eyes flashed in rage as she closed herself off to Rumaysa, who yelled as a spark of pain fizzled through her mind. She hastily stopped humming. Griselda roared in fury, breathing another wave of flames at the flying children.

The carpet dived down through the clouds. Rumaysa cried

out as she almost lost her grip on Sara, and Suleiman's brown face paled with fear.

'How do we get rid of it?' he yelled, his eyes blurring as the wind viciously whipped at them. Below, the vast lakes and forests were a blue-and-green blur.

'I don't know!' Rumaysa shouted back. 'The dragon won't listen to my song!' She screamed as the carpet took another dive. A wave of heat filled the air as Griselda shot her fiery blaze at them. This time, they were not so lucky.

The trail of flames caught one end of carpet and it jerked, spiralling uncontrollably as the back edge of the rug became engulfed. They cried out as they lost their grip and fell, spinning down towards the earth, screaming as they plummeted.

They landed in a lake with a loud splash.

Rumaysa gasped for air as water blurred her vision. She coughed and choked as she desperately tried to stay afloat, struggling to breathe. She didn't know how to swim – she was going to drown!

'Rumaysa, the carpet!' Suleiman cried from nearby.

She barely had a moment to register what he had said before the carpet appeared above her head. Desperately flinging out a hand, she managed to grab on to its edge, letting it pull her towards the shore. She collapsed on to the earth, choking up water as the carpet went back for Suleiman, who was trying to stay afloat with Sara.

Rumaysa was busy coughing on the ground when she heard two loud thuds beside her. Sara and Suleiman had tumbled off the carpet, gasping for breath.

'What. Is. Going. ON?' Sara spluttered, finally fully awake. Being thrown into a lake and nearly drowning would do that to someone.

A loud screech echoed as another tunnel of fire came barrelling towards the magic carpet, engulfing the remaining half in flames. Suleiman looked on in horror as his beloved carpet was burned to ashes before his own eyes.

'We need to hide!' Rumaysa said, fear sending goosebumps all over her skin. She wiped her streaming eyes and scrambled up, Suleiman and Sara following suit.

The three of them tore off towards the trees lining the edge of the lake. None of them had ever moved so fast in their life. Griselda's trail of fire just missed them as they disappeared into the wood.

The dragon dived down, skidding on the muddy ground as it tried to grab the children with its yellowed talons. Sara looked back and saw the great beast knock over several trees as it tried to swipe at them.

'Keep going!' she shouted as they ran deeper into the forest.

The dragon screeched out in anger as some of the trees fell on to its clawed foot. It kicked them off furiously and launched into the air, but the trees were tall and thick with leaves, which obscured the children and blocked Griselda's view from above.

'Wait – listen,' Suleiman said, stumbling to a halt.

Rumaysa and Sara slowed, straining their ears. They could hear the dragon flapping its great wings, but it sounded like Griselda was moving further away from them, until they couldn't hear her anymore.

Everyone sighed a breath of relief.

Rumaysa sat down on a log, hanging her head in her hands. Nearby, Sara took several deep breaths. Her heart thundered away in her chest – she had no idea what was going on. As she breathed in the fresh forest air, bits of her memories began to slot into place. The glass breaking – the dragon – the red eyes. She gasped with realization.

'Where are we?' she demanded, looking at Suleiman and Rumaysa.

'We're in the mountains of Hind,' Suleiman replied. 'It's not so far from Farisia . . . if you can fly.' His face crumpled and tears welled in his eyes.

'I'm sorry about your carpet,' Rumaysa said softly. She knew what it felt like to have something you treasured so dearly taken away.

'But – what am I doing here?' Sara spluttered. 'Who are you people?'

'I'm Rumaysa; that's Suleiman,' Rumaysa said, introducing them again. 'We found you at the top of a mountain. We're trying to get you back to your family.'

'My parents!' Sara cried desperately. 'Are they OK?'

Suleiman wiped his eyes as Rumaysa looked at him helplessly. 'Yes, um, the King and Queen are being kept in the dungeons by the new King Azra.'

Sara's stomach sank. She remembered hearing her parents talk about Azra. 'I don't understand,' she said faintly, her head spinning. 'How long was I asleep for? All I remember is seeing those red eyes and then everything went black.'

'Almost five months, Your Highness,' Suleiman replied softly.

Sara's green eyes bulged. 'Five months? Five *months?* I need to get back to my parents immediately!'

Rumaysa looked at Suleiman. 'How long will it take to get back there?'

He shrugged uncertainly. 'On foot? Days, maybe.'

'We need to go now, then,' Sara said decisively. '*Months!* I can't believe it – that evil Dragon Man!'

Rumaysa sighed, holding back tired and angry tears that threatened to swell in her eyes. This was not what she wanted to do.

Sara noticed the other girl's discomfort. 'What's the matter with you?' She really meant well, but Sara was a princess who'd had very little interaction with people who weren't her servants. At best, her tone could be blunt.

Rumaysa bristled. 'Nothing.'

Sara was taken aback, not used to being spoken to like that. She frowned. 'Well, let's get moving. We haven't got time to waste!'

Who made her boss? Rumaysa thought, irritated.

'Maybe we should rest for a while first,' Suleiman suggested hesitantly. He was exhausted and quite upset about his carpet. He wanted nothing more than to find a private corner and cry. 'It'll take us days to get back to

Farisia, but we won't get far like this.'

'We can't just sit here and rest!' Sara protested loudly. 'My parents are in danger! Farisia is in danger!'

Rumaysa stifled a yawn. 'I can't think of walking right now. My whole body hurts. We need to rest for a little while, at least.'

Sara felt shocked. 'Well, fine. You two can sit here, but I won't.' She turned away from them and marched off in a random direction, desperate to do *something*.

'You don't even know where you're going!' Suleiman called. 'Princess, please. We will go, but just give us a bit of time!'

Sara faltered, pausing her angry steps. All the things she had studied with her tutors had never prepared her for something like this. She didn't even know where she was.

The young princess was overcome with emotion. She had been kidnapped by a terrifying dragon, put in a cursed sleep for five months, and now she was completely helpless, in the middle of nowhere with two strangers. She had no coins, no horse, no guards . . . Anything could happen out here.

Suddenly, her parents' paranoia about leaving the palace made sense to her. After all her years of longing to be outside, in that moment Sara wanted nothing more than to be home, safe inside the palace walls. Overwhelmed, she found a big tree to hide behind before bursting into tears.

Suleiman and Rumaysa shared a look. Rumaysa sighed and hurried after Suleiman towards Sara.

'Don't cry, Princess,' Suleiman said awkwardly.

Sara sobbed. 'I just want to go home!'

'We will soon – don't worry,' Rumaysa said, trying to sound soothing. 'After we rest, we'll be able to move quicker.'

'Let's get a fire going – we'll feel better when we're dry and warm,' Suleiman said.

'I don't want a fire; I want to go home!' Sara cried angrily.

'Well, we don't want to die from cold, so we're going to get a fire going,' Rumaysa replied, irked.

Sara stared after her in shock as the other girl walked away with Suleiman. She did not like being spoken to like this.

She studied the soiled blue dress and slightly askew silver hijab Rumaysa was wearing, as though she had just come from a party or something. Suleiman wore a blue khamis that was embroidered with a popular Farisian print she recognized, but perhaps the girl wasn't from Farisia, given she was being so rude to the Princess.

She watched the two of them pile the sticks together between a cluster of trees and try to light them. Eventually, a spark ignited and a small fire flickered to life.

'Come over, then, or you're going to freeze,' Rumaysa said.

Sara hesitantly got up to go and sit with the other two. They each leaned back against a tree, exhausted. After a while, Sara turned to Suleiman and asked, 'So, what's happened to Farisia?'

Suleiman looked surprise. 'You . . . care about what's happened to Farisia?'

Sara looked back at him incredulously. 'Of course I do – they're my people!'

'But nobody has ever seen you before, nor have they seen your parents for a very long time,' Suleiman said.

Sara faltered. 'Well, my parents always say it's safer for me inside the palace – that the outside world is a dangerous place.'

Rumaysa was immediately transported back to her tower, trapped with Cordelia telling her the same thing. She shook herself to come back out of the memory, closing her eyes, grateful for the feeling of warmth on her skin and wet clothes. What she wouldn't give to be back with Ayla in her safe, cosy attic.

'My parents *want* me to go outside,' Suleiman grumbled to himself, closing his eyes as well. They were all quiet for a moment, pondering how different life could be.

'I'm really hungry,' Rumaysa proclaimed suddenly.

'Me too,' Sara said as her stomach gave a loud grumble. 'I haven't eaten in a *long* time!' She caught Rumaysa's eye and they shared a tentative smile.

'Should we find some food?' Rumaysa asked.

Suleiman made a strange noise, which Rumaysa took for a yes, but when she looked closer, it looked like he'd already fallen asleep.

'That's a good idea,' Sara said.

They headed off to find something edible and eventually came across some plums. They picked as many as they could carry and took them back to the campfire.

Suleiman stirred when they returned. 'You found food?' he asked eagerly, lurching from his seat.

They divided the fruit between them and sat back down.

'We won't be able to walk in the dark like this,' Suleiman said, yawning again.

'Perhaps we should sleep the night here and set off again early in the morning,' Sara said in a resigned voice. Though she had been asleep for months and was desperate to get to her parents, she could see how tired the other two were. Rumaysa and Suleiman looked weathered and worn.

The trio ate their small dinner quietly in front of the crackling fire. As quiet descended upon them, they listened out for any sound of the dragon, but the air was still, save for the wind whistling through the trees. It felt like an odd moment of refuge, and the three of them took the opportunity to close their eyes again, just for a moment.

A loud screech echoed in the air. It felt to Sara that they had only been asleep for minutes, but the sky was already pitch black. There was another roar, and Rumaysa and Suleiman jolted awake too.

'She's back,' Sara said fearfully, jumping up.

The other two scrambled to their feet, looking up at the sky. A great shadow flew overhead.

'We should move,' Rumaysa said in a low voice.

Suleiman pulled something small and gold out of his damp sock. It was a compass.

'Farisia is south of Hind, so we just have to head . . .' He set the compass down on the ground and waited for the needle to settle. 'This way!' he said, gesturing deeper into the woods.

'Let's go,' Sara said, marching off in that direction. Suleiman followed, trying not roll his eyes. The Princess was definitely a leader, at least.

Sara led the way, constantly looking up at the sky. Every now and again they could see a shadow circling above, but the dragon seemed to be none the wiser about where in the forest they were.

Sara looked around as the trio walked in companionable silence, taking in her surroundings, drinking in the outside world after so many years inside the palace. It was wonderful to feel something different than the palace floors under her feet.

'Does it feel weird being outside?' Suleiman asked Sara curiously, after a while.

'Not really,' Sara said, pretending she felt braver than she did. 'It is nice to be on my own adventure.'

'What were you doing in the palace all this time, then?' he pressed.

Sara shrugged. 'I was tutored. I played with the staff and explored the palace a lot. My parents were always worried something bad would happen to me out here. But I think they're just a bit too protective.'

'There are always bad things wherever you go,' Suleiman said. 'But there are good things, too. Take Rumaysa, for instance: she was locked in a tower but then she got out and now we're friends. So, good and bad, right?' He looked at Rumaysa with an earnest smile.

Rumaysa smiled back. 'Yes – good and bad.'

'You were locked in a tower?' Sara repeated, staring at Rumaysa with wide eyes. 'Why?'

Rumaysa spent the next few minutes filling her in on her life in the tower, the Witch and her escape.

'Wow, and you escaped by yourself? How brave!' Sara said with a pang of jealousy.

Above them, the dragon screeched, louder than before. Suleiman jerked as a shadow passed over their heads. They froze, but the dragon carried on flying, its screeches getting further away.

'It's still looking for us,' Suleiman said, shivering.

'Let's keep moving,' Sara said, quickening her pace.

Dawn was breaking across the forest of Hind, searing pinks and blues lighting the morning sky. The trio were exhausted, but Griselda still loomed above them. Sara was about suggest they stop for a rest, but as she opened her mouth she caught an odd scent on the air. 'Er, can anyone else smell that?'

'Smell what?' said Rumaysa and Suleiman together.

'It smells like . . . burning,' Sara replied slowly. All three of them sniffed and caught a distinct smell of burning wood.

'It's coming from behind,' Rumaysa said, looking back as a familiar loud screech rang overhead.

'The dragon!' Suleiman cried.

They saw tendrils of black smoke snaking through the air and a flickering of orange in the distance.

'It's trying to smoke us out!' Sara said, horrified.

'We need to run!' Suleiman yelled.

The three of them tore off, stumbling as they fought to keep their footing on the uneven forest floor.

Above them, sunlight was beginning to stream through the thick canopy of trees as another terrifying screech sounded in the air.

'She's getting close!' Sara shouted.

Suleiman was panting hard. 'We can't keep running!'

Swathes of forest behind them had disappeared into smoke and flame, but ahead of them the trees were beginning to thin out. The children stumbled into a clearing, gasping for breath. The air was clearer here, but it meant that the chase was over: Griselda could finally see them. She gave a triumphant roar and a ball of fire came barrelling towards where they had been just a few moments ago.

'Hide!' Rumaysa hissed.

The three of them leaped behind different trees, crouching down as the dragon tried to zero in on them.

'Rumaysa, is there anything you can do?' Suleiman whispered.

Rumaysa looked back at him, panicked. 'It doesn't respond to my magic!'

'Try again!' he begged as the dragon swooped down,

landing with a quaking thud on the forest floor. This time, there was no escape. Griselda growled, scouring the trees in search of the children as swells of orange-and-red fire blazed behind her.

Rumaysa was frightened. The heat from the burning trees was starting to hurt, and her skin felt hot and tight. But she had to focus. Sara and Suleiman needed her.

She closed her eyes and reached deep into her magic, letting the light soak its way through her. She held out her hands as she looked up through the trees and smoke to the dragon and tried to touch it with her magic. The dragon recoiled suddenly as if it had been burned. It roared in protest, but Rumaysa tried again, more gently this time.

Sara and Suleiman watched with wide eyes as Rumaysa stepped out from behind the tree. She was now in plain view of the dragon.

'Rumaysa, what are you doing?' Sara hissed. 'Get back!'

But Rumaysa was so deep in her own magic that she couldn't hear her. Something felt different this time.

I'm not trying to hurt you, she thought.

Griselda pulled back, trying to resist, but Rumaysa could sense the dragon's hesitance in doing so.

Sara watched in amazement as Rumaysa sang. The great beast seemed to writhe, as if to shake her song off, but Sara could see it was affecting her. There was a golden glow emanating from all around the girl as if she were a star lit up. Was she an angel?

She had a few words to say to her parents when they were all safe again – the outside world was incredible!

When Rumaysa next reached out, the dragon allowed the magic to touch her. Rumaysa sensed it lulling the dragon into a softer frame of mind.

After years of being treated viciously by Azra, Griselda was caught off guard by how *gentle* Rumaysa felt. Slowly, the great dragon lowered her head and bowed in front of the girl, her wings folding in, knocking a few trees over in the process.

Suleiman shrieked with fear, and Sara shrank back as the red eyes loomed. Rumaysa, however, smiled at the dragon. 'I mean you no harm,' she said, her voice kind and reassuring.

Griselda snorted, letting out a small trail of smoke. Her eyes, previously so fierce, gazed at Rumaysa with interest.

Rumaysa approached her slowly. Griselda let her come and didn't resist when she put a soft, chapped hand to her head and stroked her gently.

The dragon closed her eyes in pleasure.

'Are you OK?' Rumaysa asked, sensing the dragon's emotions.

Griselda blinked slowly, which Rumaysa took to mean yes.

Curiosity pulled Sara forward, while Suleiman whimpered from behind his tree. Griselda's head turned sharply as the Princess approached, and she let out a low growl.

Sara bristled. 'You *kidnapped* me!' she said.

Griselda snorted in anger and lowered her head.

'Stop,' Rumaysa said firmly.

Griselda quietened, but still looked distrustfully at Sara.

Sara marvelled at how the dragon responded to Rumaysa and wished, for a moment, that she was magic too. She inched further forward to get a better look. She really was magnificent. Griselda's scales gleamed purple from the glow of the fire behind them; she was the biggest creature Sara had ever seen.

Sara looked at Rumaysa. 'Do you think she might take us to my parents?' she asked hopefully.

Rumaysa reached out once again towards Griselda. The dragon blinked her red eyes once more.

'I think she might,' said Rumaysa, smiling.

V

Rumaysa heaved herself up on to the dragon's back and then turned to help the other two. Sara eagerly scrambled up, but Suleiman looked anxious.

'Come on,' Sara said. 'It's really not as bad as it looks.'

Suleiman looked up at her doubtfully. It took a bit of slipping and sliding, but he eventually managed to clamber on to Griselda's back. They had each barely gripped on to one of the smooth, scaly spikes protruding from her spine when the dragon launched into the air. She pushed them out of the burning trees and into the clear morning sky.

The girls cried out in delight while Suleiman clung on for dear life. He was used to flying on his magic carpet, but this felt completely different. He wasn't sure he liked it.

Sara's head swivelled from side to side as she drank in the beautiful scenery of mountain tops and lakes below her. The forest trees began to thin again as they reached the southern mountains, the landscape constantly changing. With the wind in her face and the sun above her, it felt like a dream.

The dragon soared towards Farisia, moving much quicker than the flying carpet.

'There's the palace!' Suleiman shouted after a while.

'We're here!' Sara yelled, relieved at the sight of the magnificent sapphire turrets and marble palace walls. She was finally home.

Griselda banked and began to swoop downward. The three of them screamed as she soared towards the ground, faster and faster. Just as it seemed they were about to crash, the dragon spread her wings wide to slow the descent. She snorted haughtily at the children.

Griselda landed in the courtyard with a light thud and lowered herself so they could climb off her back.

Suleiman stumbled dazedly away, but Rumaysa alighted gracefully and turned back to the magnificent dragon.

'Thank you,' she said.

Griselda gave a low growl of understanding.

'Come on,' Sara urged. 'We've got to go and save my parents!' The Princess tore off towards the palace, but before she had even reached the steps, there was a shout from a balcony.

'Griselda! What are you doing here?' It was Azra.

Griselda slowly turned her head and glared up at the man. Azra recoiled as a short burst of flame came out of her nostrils.

His eyes fell upon the three children standing beside her. '*What is all this?*' he demanded in dragon tongue. '*Is that the Princess? Why did you bring her back?*'

Griselda stood up on her hind legs and let out a huge roar, causing Azra to stumble back in surprise – the dragon had never disobeyed him before.

Azra backed away slowly as his dragon glowered at him, her menacing red eyes wide with contempt.

'What have you done to my dragon?' he demanded, looking at Sara.

'Where are my parents?' Sara shouted back.

'Be quiet you sill child,' Azra scoffed. 'You have no business speaking to your *King* in such a foul way.'

Sara scowled at him. 'You're *not* the King! And you will

pay for what you've done to my family, and to Farisia!'

Azra laughed at her. 'Guards!' he shouted. 'Take these fools and put them in the dungeon!'

Sara, Suleiman and Rumaysa backed away nervously as a number of guards sprang from the shadows. But before they could reach the children Griselda let out another low growl and a stream of fire that stopped just short of the guards. They screamed and ran back.

'*Griselda, stop this!*' Azra tried to reach out once more, but he found himself blocked as Griselda resisted his acidic touch. The dragon fumed, blowing another wreath of fire at him.

He let out a loud scream and dived behind the balcony.

'Guards! Shoot her! Shoot the dragon!' Azra shouted, jumping up to run inside.

Keeping their distance, the guards shot their arrows at Griselda, but they simply bounced off her thick, scaly skin without leaving so much as a scratch. Griselda roared, louder this time, and took another deep breath. The guards dropped their weapons and ran for cover before she'd even released the flame.

'Yes!' said Sara, punching the air. 'Brilliant work, Griselda! This way!' she called to the other two, hurrying into the palace.

Sara led them through the labyrinthine halls, and as she tore through the vast corridors, she noticed that it looked starkly different to how she'd remembered it. All the historic family portraits had been replaced with endless pictures of Azra in different outfits. Instead of armoured statues lining the corridors, there were frightening dragon sculptures and weaponry. More guards rushed past the children in the opposite direction, ignoring them as the sounds of Griselda raging in the courtyard got louder and the air grew warmer.

Eventually, they arrived at the entrance to the dungeons, which were faintly lit by small candles hanging from the stone walls. The smell of damp and must ran deep here; Sara had never been happier to breathe it in.

As she scanned the cells for her parents, Sara heard a voice that made her heart soar.

'What's going on?'

'Baba!' Sara shouted, following his voice.

'Sara?' her parents yelled.

The Princess ran down to the end of the corridor, Suleiman and Rumaysa hot on her heels. She skidded to a halt at a cell where two ragged figures stood. In the dim candlelight, she could see the tired faces of her parents, thinned from starvation and worry. The King and Queen cried out as they saw their daughter.

Sara rattled the metal bars separating her from her parents. 'How do I get you out?'

'Let me,' Rumaysa said, hurrying forward. She put her hands on the door and closed her eyes, pulsing out a golden light that melted away the lock in seconds.

The prison door swung open, and Sara and her parents rushed to embrace one another.

'Oh, my sweet girl!' Queen Shiva cried.

'I knew we'd see you again,' the King sobbed. Both he and the Queen held Sara tight.

'I'll never let you out of my sight again, I swear,' her mother said through a stream of tears.

Finally, the King wiped his eyes and stood up straight.

'Where's Azra?' he demanded, looking at Rumaysa and Suleiman.

Just then there was a scream from above.

'Er, I think he's running away from his dragon,' Suleiman said. 'Er – Your Highness,' he hastily added.

The King and Queen looked surprised, but didn't wait. Everybody followed after them as they headed back upstairs, and when they emerged from the dungeons it became clear that the palace was in flames.

'Outside, quick!' the Queen said, ushering the children. Coughing and spluttering, they all ran into the courtyard. Moments later, Azra came running out too, wildly flapping at his bottom, where there was a small fire crackling.

Griselda was wild. She was lashing her tail and breathing fire across the whole courtyard, and it seemed that the sight of Azra had enraged her even more. Everyone was desperately trying to avoid both the crackling flames and her deadly tail.

The King and Queen stopped in their tracks at the sight of her.

'What is she doing?' the Queen asked, staring in horror.

Azra ran past them, trying to get to the palace gates, but Griselda blocked him off with another wave of fire.

Azra turned back round, flailing. 'Somebody help me!'

The King marched up to Azra, ready to throttle him. Queen Shiva was right beside him, livid.

'I will throw you in the dungeon for the rest of your days!' she roared.

'Now, now – let's not be hasty,' Azra said quickly, backing away from them. He had to stop before he ended up in the fire consuming the gates. 'Your Majesties, *please*,' Azra beseeched them. 'I-I never meant to—'

'Steal our thrones? Kidnap our daughter?' the King offered angrily. A large vein on his forehead was throbbing menacingly.

'I-I – well . . .' He fumbled for an excuse, but was cut off by another screech from Griselda.

'Get back,' Sara said urgently, pulling her parents out of the way. The King and Queen jumped back hastily as Griselda looked at Azra, her angry red eyes glowing.

Azra tried to look away, but stood rooted to the spot, as if hypnotized. 'No – wait – Griselda –' he started to say, but suddenly his lips could no longer move. His eyelids drooped and his knees gave way, and he fell to the ground, unconscious, in his own cursed sleep.

'Griselda, you did it!' Rumaysa said, running towards the dragon. The dragon puffed a ring of smoke out of her nostrils in triumph.

'What's happened to him?' the King asked, looking in shock between Azra and the dragon.

'She put him to sleep,' Sara said with some familiarity. She gave the dragon a wry smile as Griselda lowered her body, drooping her head so Rumaysa could pat her.

'Well done, girl,' Rumaysa said, stroking her warm scales.

Griselda huffed and stood. She held her head back and let out a powerful roar, causing everybody to cover their ears as her cry echoed through the kingdom. The dragon stalked towards Azra's sleeping body and picked him up with her great talons. She let out another strong cry as she launched into the air, nearly causing Rumaysa's hijab to fly off from the force of the wind.

Sara joined her parents near the charred palace gates, Rumaysa and Suleiman just behind her. The Queen pulled her daughter into another hug and cried softly into Sara's curly hair, exhausted. 'You'll sleep in our room from now on – I don't care!'

'And I'm going to have you trained to fight in battle,' the King said fervently, hugging them both.

Sara felt overwhelmed with joy to be reunited with her parents. She embraced them happily, feeling safe and warm in their arms despite the chaos that continued to unfold around them. Flames leaped up around the palace, casting an orange glow across their faces.

'But Mama, Baba, I had such an adventure outside!' Sara

said excitedly. 'There's so much more out there to see!'

'Absolutely not!' Queen Shiva protested, pulling back. 'You are not leaving this palace ever again!'

'Isn't the palace kind of ruined?' Suleiman whispered to Rumaysa.

She nodded as they looked back at the half-destroyed flaming building.

'Mother, you can't keep me locked up! And clearly the palace isn't indestructible, either!' Sara said, motioning towards it with her hand. 'Think of all those people out there! They're *our* people, and they don't even know us! We don't know *them*! Maybe if we'd had a better relationship with them, they wouldn't have tried to overthrow us.'

The King seemed to consider his daughter's words for a moment. Sara braced herself for his anger.

'You're right, Sara.'

Sara froze in surprise. 'I am?'

Queen Shiva's face softened a little. 'It's a cruel world out there, Sara. We are just trying to protect you.'

'I know, Mother,' Sara said. 'But not everyone is so cruel. There's good and bad.' She smiled at Suleiman.

He beamed back.

210

While the royal family had been talking, the people of Farisia had rushed towards the palace. They had heard all the noise, of course, and soon everybody was dashing forward to help quell the flames. The King and Queen joined their people in passing buckets and throwing water, and as the fire died down, a crowd began to gather around them. For the first time in years, the people of Farisia saw their rulers standing among them. They could not believe their eyes.

'What happened to Azra?' came a shout from the crowd.

Everybody shared a look.

'The dragon dealt with him,' Queen Shiva announced with a satisfied smile.

The crowd cheered in response. The King and Queen smiled at their subjects as they pressed around, as close as they could, desperate to get a good look at their royal family. They could see how worn and starved their King and Queen looked and were fascinated to see Princess Sara for the first time. She was almost the spitting image of her mother, though she had the King's nose.

'Why did you abandon us?' somebody else called.

A silence fell across the crowd.

The King and Queen looked at each other uncomfortably. Everybody stared at them, waiting.

'We just wanted to protect our daughter,' the Queen eventually said. 'We thought the best thing was to keep her safe inside the palace. But Azra managed to take her regardless.'

'Will you leave us again?' yet another called.

The King looked at his people shamefacedly. 'My people, I am sorry. We have not been just rulers. The way you all came together to help put out the palace fire was more than we deserved, I dare say.'

'We will change our ways,' the Queen promised.

'How can we trust you?' a voice demanded.

The King and Queen shared another uncomfortable look.

'I will make sure of it,' Sara said, speaking for the first time to her people. Her voice was bold and brave; even her parents were taken aback. 'I know you all don't know me, but if I am to rule Farisia one day I would like to get to know you all.'

The people of Farisia cheered, and the King promised an assembly the next day in the village square so he could outline his new plans for a fairer and more just Farisia.

As the crowd dispersed, Sara was left to be engulfed by her parents once more.

'Perhaps you don't need all that extra training to become queen,' King Emad said, looking in wonder at his daughter. 'It seems you are already very well acquainted with how a good ruler should behave. I know I haven't set the best example.'

Rumaysa looked at Sara and smiled. Despite the fact that she hadn't yet found her own parents, she was starting to appreciate how good it felt to help other people.

'Suleiman?' A tall woman wearing a purple hijab and cloak came forward from the last of the dispersing crowd. A short man followed behind her, looking just as concerned. 'What's happened? You found the Princess?' she said excitedly.

'Mother, Father, these are my friends, Rumaysa and Princess Sara,' he said gesturing at the girls. 'Rumaysa found the Princess and woke her up from her sleep.'

'She did?' his father said, looking crestfallen.

'Suleiman helped too,' Rumaysa added.

'He's an adventurous explorer, Your Majesties,' Suleiman's mother said quickly, putting an arm round her son. 'He's always running around looking for new places to discover.'

Suleiman shrugged his mother's arm off and turned to look at her. 'Mother, *you* were the one who wanted me to find the Princess,' he said. 'I like being indoors and making things. All

I want to do right now is make another carpet.'

Suleiman's parents turned red.

'You like making things, do you, boy?' Queen Shiva asked. 'Well, we shall see to it that you are sent to the finest school where you can learn to make whatever you desire.'

Suleiman's eyes nearly fell out of his head. 'Really? I would love that!'

'Oh no, Your Majesty – that's too much!' his father said, shocked. 'Really, he's an adventurous boy – there's no need for that!'

'No, Father, I want to go to school and learn!' Suleiman said.

'But all those silly inventions won't do any good,' his father said flippantly. 'You need to learn to be a real man, out there making a name for yourself.'

'I don't want to be a "real man" – whatever *that* is – I just want to be me!' Suleiman said firmly. 'I'm not going on any more adventures or finding missing princesses or whatever else you think I should do. *I* am going to decide who *I'm* going to be.'

His parents were taken aback. Sometimes, it was all too easy for adults to decide what was 'right' for their children. Though Suleiman's parents may have meant well, they didn't always know what was best for themselves, let alone their child.

'We will also ensure you receive ten thousand gold coins for helping find our daughter,' the Queen added. 'If you need a place to work, young man, you are most welcome at our home.'

'Thank you so much,' Suleiman said gratefully.

'Come, Suleiman – we should get you home and cleaned up,' his mother said. 'A thousand thank-yous, Your Majesties.' She curtseyed.

Suleiman looked to Sara and bowed. 'Princess, it was an honour.'

'Thanks, Suleiman,' Sara said. 'Maybe we can go exploring together some time? We don't have to go too far, though,' she added with a smile.

'I'd love that,' the boy responded eagerly, before turning to Rumaysa. 'I really hope you find your parents. I'll be praying for you.'

'Thanks, Suleiman. Maybe I'll see you around at the next tower,' she said, grinning.

Suleiman's face fell. 'I hope not – I just want to sit in my house for a year.'

Sara and Rumaysa laughed, and Suleiman allowed himself to be led away by his parents, turning to wave over his shoulder at the two girls.

'What's this about your parents, dear?' the King asked.

Before Rumaysa could reply, Sara animatedly started to fill her parents in about Rumaysa's upbringing.

'You poor thing!' the Queen cried, aghast.

'I could help you find your parents, if you'd like?' Sara offered to Rumaysa.

Rumaysa's heart swelled with hope, just as the necklace gave a familiar tug from round her neck. She pulled it out and saw it was glowing bright purple. She sighed inwardly.

Was it calling her to another person who needed her help? Perhaps that was just what she was meant to do.

'I have to go,' Rumaysa said reluctantly. 'But thank you.'

'Where will you go?' asked Sara.

'Wherever I'm taken to, I suppose,' Rumaysa said. 'It was good meeting you, Sara.'

'Why don't you go to Splinterfell, dear?' the Queen said. 'Rumaysa is a very Splinterfellian name.'

'Yes, it is,' the King agreed eagerly.

'Splinterfell?' Rumaysa said hopefully. The necklace tugged

at her again, more urgently. 'Thank you! I'll try going there –
thank you!'

'Thank you for saving me!' Sara replied, pulling Rumaysa
in for a big hug. 'I'll miss you!'

Rumaysa hugged her back fondly. 'I'll miss you too.
Hopefully we'll see each other again, one day.'

Sara smiled widely at her. 'Yes, please. If you ever need
anyone to join you on an adventure, I'll be there.'

Behind their daughter, the King and Queen exchanged a
worried look.

Rumaysa laughed and bid the royal family farewell. The
necklace continued to tug at her, and she closed her hand
round it, hoping and praying that it would take her to
Splinterfell.

She wanted nothing more than to be with her parents, but
she had a feeling the necklace had other ideas.

And so Rumaysa made a vow to herself. She would find her
parents. And she would help anyone she could along the way.

Wistfully, Sara watched Rumaysa go, hoping one day she
could walk off towards her own adventures. Eventually, she
turned to her parents and asked, 'So, where are we sleeping
tonight?'

The palace of Farisia was ruined, so the royal family were taken to the nearest inn while their home was repaired. They were put up in the finest rooms, and Sara quickly became good friends with the innkeepers and their children. Her days at the inn were some of the happiest of her life so far.

It became clear to the King and Queen that keeping their daughter hidden away had done nothing for her safety or her happiness, nor for their reputation.

During their stay, the townspeople came to the inn to give gifts to the royal family. King Emad and Queen Shiva realized with shame how much they had abandoned their people.

The people of Farisia were glad that Azra no longer ruled them, but they also told the King and Queen that they wanted change. And finally – with the help of their daughter – King Emad and Queen Shiva were ready to rule.

Sara knew that one day her time would come too, where she would have to guide her people through the good and the bad. It used to seem like a faraway dream, something she could never do. But now, seeing her parents flourish and the kingdom excel, Sara realized nothing was impossible, especially with the help of a few friends.

THE END

ACKNOWLEDGEMENTS

The biggest thank-you to Alice Sutherland-Hawes, my stellar agent, for believing in me from the beginning.

A huge thank-you also to Lucy Pearse, who saw something in *Rumaysa* and gave me the chance to tell this story.

To my incredible editor, Cate Augustin: thank you so much for your endless wisdom, support and enthusiasm. Your vision and expertise helped me get the best out of this book and I couldn't have done it without you.

Thank you to Areeba Siddique for the cover illustration and Rhaida El Touny for the inside illustrations.

To the wonderful team at Macmillan Children's Books, thank you for all your hard work. Rachel Vale, for the beautiful cover design, Tracey Ridgewell for text design, Sarah Clarke in Sales and Rachel Graves in International Sales. Ruth Brooks and the joyous Katie Bradburn in Trade Marketing, my publicist Sabina Maharjan and Cheyney Smith in Marketing.

Thank you to my copyeditor Vron Lyons and proofreader Sam Stanton Stewart.

Rumaysa is an ode to some of my favourite fairytales, but the friendships in this book are a testament to the incredible people in my life who have always encouraged me to pursue my dreams – my first ever readers who read anything and everything I sent them: Bushra, Mariam, Naomisha and Naznin. A huge thank-you to Zainab who once wrote 'Rapunzel, let down your hijab' on a dinner-party board and is always on hand to advise on anything literary.

Thank you to Nadine, Nida, Shahla and Sumi for always championing my work and for a friendship that has saved me in more ways than one.

Thank you also to Sara Adams, Amy Perkins and Frances Gough for their expert advice and unwavering support.

A thank-you to my parents for all that they did to give us the best chance in life (and buying me books as a child even when things were tight and taking me to the library to get even more books).

Thank you to my husband for making fairytales happen in real life too.

And to you, reader, thank you for reading this book.

ABOUT THE AUTHOR

Radiya Hafiza studied English Language and Literature at King's College London and worked in publishing for a few years. Radiya grew up reading classic Western fairy tales that never had any brown girls in them – *Rumaysa* is her debut novel, bringing such stories to children who need to see themselves represented.

ABOUT THE ILLUSTRATOR

Rhaida El Touny is an illustrator and graphic designer based in The Hague. Drawing has been her passion from an early age, and much of her art explores life as a Muslim woman in a global cultural context. She mainly draws portraits of strong young women of colour who inspire her, with a focus on diversity and female empowerment.